MW00945492

# Kurtain Motel

## Sin Series Book 1

Written by A. I. Nasser
Edited by Emma Salam and Lance Piao

Thank You and Bonus Novel!

To really show you my appreciation for purchasing this book, **I'd love to send you a full-length horror novel in 3 formats (MOBI, EPUB and PDF) absolutely free!** This will surely make chills run down your spine!

Download your full-length horror novel, get free short stories, and receive future discounts by visiting www.ScareStreet.com/AINasser

See you in the shadows,
A.I. Nasser

# Kurtain Motel

## Prologue

Alexander Pike burst through the doors of the small diner just as the rain began to pick up. The storm had caught up with him. The warnings on the radio were a bleak memory of the beginning of his journey when he had ignored the meteorologists. After all, he was Alexander Pike, and no storm would stop him from getting where he needed to be.

Alex shook the rain off his suit jacket and brushed his fingers through his hair. He had misjudged the weather, but it didn't matter. He would wait in the diner until the worst of it was past and then be on his way again. He was on a tight deadline, and he doubted the storm would keep him here for very long.

He walked over to the bar and pushed up onto an empty stool, barely taking in his surroundings as he pulled out his cellphone. He had no coverage, and he cursed his luck. He would have to find another way to call San Francisco. Slipping out of his jacket, he folded it neatly and draped it over the back of his stool. He sniffed as his sinuses filled with the smell of bacon and eggs coming from the kitchen beyond.

There were very few  people in the diner this time of the night, which wasn't much of a surprise. The weather forecast had been bleak for a few days now, and people had been advised to stay indoors and wait out the storm. Alex barely registered the petite blonde waitress napping in one of the stalls or the old gentleman at the other end of the bar cradling his coffee in both hands. Although Alex was known to be reckless, a trait that had proven valuable at times and tiresome at others, he doubted many people would venture out in this weather.

"What can I get you?"

Alex turned to face the middle-aged woman, her green eyes boring into him as she wiped her hands on a towel hanging from her waist. She was pretty in a back-country sort of way, her hair tied back in a tight ponytail that allowed her high cheekbones to stand out. She was smiling at him, but the gesture seemed more strained than genuine, and Alex could immediately tell that the woman would rather be somewhere else other than here.

Alex grabbed at the small menu laid out before him and quickly scanned it, his eyes flying over the specials before he found his poison.

"Coffee. Black."

The woman nodded and turned away, leaving Alex to brood over his phone as he turned it off and restarted it, hoping for a signal. His eyes caught a movement to his left and he looked up to see an old man watching him closely, eyes intent as he sipped slowly at his drink. The lights in the diner flickered with the resonant sounds of thunder outside, and the rain increased in fury.

There would be no calling out tonight. The storm wasn't letting up, and it would be hours before he could jump back into his Beamer and be back on his way. Deciding on a more comfortable seat, Alex stood up and settled into one of the booths near the window, looking out at the falling rain in dismay. His car was the only vehicle in the lot, which struck him as strange given that he was not the only guest in the diner.

The woman at the bar called out to the waitress and Alex watched in amusement as the girl trudged to pick up his drink and bring it to him. She set it down slowly, hands shaking, and Alex could tell from the black rings under her eyes that she was in dire need of a good night's sleep. He remembered his earlier days working the night shift in a call center downtown, how the highlight of his day would be the moment his head settled onto his pillow and his eyes shut out the world around him.

"Thank you," Alex said softly, eyeing the waitress as she grunted and walked back to her booth, immediately settling down again. He watched her, and his eyes moved back to the old man who was still staring intently at him. It was starting to make Alex eerily uncomfortable, and he toyed with the idea of calling the man out and embarrassing him in front of everyone.

*Forget it.*

Alex shook his head and stared back out the window. He wrapped both hands around the coffee mug, letting the heat seep into his skin and warm him up. He hadn't noticed how cold he was until this moment, and he gently raised the cup to his mouth to take a sip.

The old man slid into the booth, startling Alex.

"Jesus, what's the matter with you?" Alex gasped, frowning irritably.

The old man gave him a toothless smile and pointed a shaky finger at Alex.

"I know you," he said, his voice raspy from one too many cigarettes, his tongue licking his lips as he spoke.

"I highly doubt that," Alex replied, glancing at the bar and hoping to get the waitress's attention. The woman had disappeared into the kitchen, though, and all Alex could hear was her soft humming as food sizzled on the grill inside.

"Sure I do," the old man said. "I saw your face on one of 'em magazines o'er there."

Alex turned to where the man was pointing and saw the front cover of TIME magazine. A large portrait of him filled the cover, hiding the magazine's title behind his sleek hair. Alex remembered the interview clearly, and the woman he had seduced into his bed after she was done asking him questions. It had been a fruitful day.

"That's you, ain't it?" the old man asked.

Alex looked back at the man, taking in the thin, long greying hair and the stubble that was interrupted by patches of skin. The man smiled at him, what remained of his teeth yellow and rotten against his pale skin. The only thing worse than his attire, was the pungent smell coming out of his mouth.

"Maybe," Alex said, trying to breathe through his mouth.

The old man shook his finger at him. "Ah, ah, Mr. Time Magazine," he chuckled. "Don't be so modest."

Alex sighed. "Do you want an autograph?"

The man laughed hard and smacked his hand on the table. "That would be somethin', now won't it?"

Alex patted his shirt for a pen and began reaching for his coat when the old man stopped him.

"No, Mr. Pike," the man said, his tone more serious. "What I want you to do is confess."

Alex frowned. "Confess?"

The old man leaned in and gestured for Alex to come closer. Alex hesitated, then obliged.

"You see, I know where your millions came from, Mr. Pike," the old man whispered. "Between you and me, I really don't care much for the thousands y' scammed into trustin' you with their hard-earned savings. If you want to throw your money away, no one's stoppin' ya, is what I always say."

Alex pulled back in anger. "Listen, I don't know who you think you are, but you've got your facts all wrong."

The old man held up a hand and stopped Alex from continuing. "Don't care. I know what I know. All you need to do is confess, and we can all be on our merry way."

"Confess what?"

"That you're a thief, Mr. Pike," the old man grinned. "That you're a thief and a coward, and that all this publicity 'round's ya is nothin' but show. You ain't got a dime of all dat money left, do ya? That gamblin' problem of yours, a real bitch if y'ask me."

Alex opened his mouth to say something, but the words failed him. He had no idea who this man was, or how he had come to know all that he knew. All Alex did know was that he didn't have to sit around and listen to the old man rant.

Looking out the window, Alex could see the rain letting up. He pulled out a hundred dollar bill from his wallet, threw it on the table and began to stand up. The old man reached out a gnarled hand to stop him, which Alex quickly slapped away.

"Don't," Alex hissed. "I don't know who you are, but what you're doing is called harassment, and I could have you arrested right here, right now." Alex grabbed his coat and pulled it on, keeping his eyes on the old man and the ridiculous grin on his face.

"No one leaves until they've confessed," the old man said, his voice barely audible even in the silence of the diner. "Ask 'round. They'll all tell ya."

Suddenly the diner was full of people, crammed together, shoulder to shoulder as they stood limp and motionless. Men and women varying in age and size, eyes downcast and shoulders slumped with their lips moving as if in silent prayer. Alex felt something cold touch his hand, and his head snapped back to the old man.

Only, he wasn't old anymore, and the hollow eyes staring up at Alex made his blood curl.

"They want their money back, Alex."

Alex pulled away from the man, quickly barging through the crowd of people, pushing past them towards the diner door. The rain outside was falling in torrents again, but Alex didn't care. He needed to get out, now. The sudden urgency was overwhelming as he felt hands grab at the nape of his neck and the collar of his shirt.

Alex pushed through the diner door, hands stretched out to break his fall as he anticipated the rough texture of asphalt and water. He hit the ground hard, his knees slamming against the floor sending bolts of pain up his spine, and when he looked up, he found that he was still in the diner.

Dozens of eyes stared at him, and as the mob of people moved forward in unison, hands stretched out, voices rising, Alex began to scream.

## Chapter 1

Patrick Lahm knew he was in trouble the minute the gas light began flashing. He glanced in frustration at the marker poised dangerously under the E, and slammed his fist against the steering wheel. His mind raced as he tried to remember how many more miles he had left before his car would shut down on him. When he couldn't retrieve the information, he slowed down and stopped by the curb.

'Route 25' was empty.

Patrick turned off the ignition, hoping to save what little gas he had left, and stepped out of the car. He glanced up and down the highway, hoping to see twin beacons of headlights from either side, but was rewarded with nothing but emptiness. He slammed his palm against the driver's door, wondering what the hell he had been thinking when he had driven past the last gas station several miles back.

"Smart, hot shot, really smart," he mumbled to himself.

Patrick made his way to the trunk and opened it, rummaging through its contents as he searched for the spare gas canister he usually left aside for instances like these. When he couldn't find it, he slammed the trunk closed.

"Perfect," he sighed. "Just perfect!"

Patrick opened the back door and pulled a map out of his laptop bag. He laid it out on the hood of the car and angled it enough for the light to help him make out where he was. The next town was at least twenty miles north, and there was no way he was going to be able to walk that. He traced a finger along the highway's blue line, squinting as he tried to find a gas station nearby. He remembered how the woman at his last stop had assured him the map would be a life saver, but right now it was telling him to just call it a day and sleep in the car. Maybe the morning traffic would send him a savior.

Patrick glanced at his watch. It was just past midnight, and he had to be in Hartford by noon. Even if he could wait it out until the morning, there was no way he would make it to the book signing in time. Patrick folded the map and replaced it, slinging the laptop bag over his shoulder and locking the car.

He would just have to risk the walk and hope someone would pick him up on the way.

\*\*\*

It was only two miles and three pairs of headlights later when a car finally stopped for Patrick. He didn't try to get its attention, the frustration of having had failed three times reminded him how little people trusted hitchhikers. So, it was a surprise when the driver of the Chevrolet pulled up to the curb in front of Patrick and turned on the emergency lights.

Patrick picked up the pace and leaned in through the passenger door window, instantly relieved when the smiling face of a priest gazed back at him. The man was still wearing his parish clothes, the white band around his collar clear beneath the large brown overcoat around his shoulders. He looked barely over fifty, a day-old stubble framing his jaw and only adding to the man's handsome features. The cold had already begun setting in, and hot air was blasting out of the air conditioner.

"Where ya headed?" the priest asked, his voice soft as if he were taking confession.

"Anywhere that has a phone," Patrick replied. He could already feel the beginnings of a drizzle. "My car broke down a few miles back, and I need to reach Triple A."

The priest's smile widened as he nodded. "Cell reception is not what it seems out here."

Patrick shrugged. "I wouldn't know. My phone died hours ago."

A wind picked up and started blowing the rain into Patrick's face, forcing him to squint.

"Well, get on in," the priest waved at him. "You don't want to be caught out in the open in this weather."

Patrick thanked him and quickly slid into the passenger seat, rolling up the window as the priest idled out into the highway and picked up speed.

Patrick warmed his hands against the hot gusts coming out from between the slits in the dashboard, letting the warm

7

air soothe him. "I didn't know it was going to rain," he said nonchalantly, looking up at the priest.

The man smiled, yet kept his eyes on the road. "Connecticut weather can fool ya if ya let it." He looked at Patrick and winked.

"Thanks for this, by the way," Patrick said, rubbing his hands together for more warmth.

"Don't mention it," the priest replied. "What kind of man of God would I be if I had let you walk in this rain?" He looked at Patrick seriously. "You're not crazy, are you?"

Patrick coughed laughter as the priest eased into his own bemused smile.

"So, where?"

"Hartford," Patrick said. "I have a book signing tomorrow. Though from the look of things, I might just miss it."

"An author, eh?" the priest smiled. "Anything I might have read?"

"Doubtful," Patrick replied. "They're not the holiest of works."

The priest chuckled. "We all have our guilty pleasures."

Patrick looked at the man and smiled, wondering what a priest was doing driving down Route 25 at two in the morning. It was one of those questions that he usually kept to himself, the timeless what-if's of any author. What if the priest was actually in disguise and was going to kill him? What if the man was on a calling to save the damned?

*Daydreams,* Patrick thought to himself. *Daydreams that eventually turned into stories.*

If he could write them.

Ever since his last bestseller, he had hit a speed bump in the road of creativity. At least, that's what he liked to call it. His editor liked to call it a wall. Either way, the block was costing him money and time, and although the publishers had hinted at using a ghostwriter to help him churn out another book, Patrick had fought hard against the idea.

The priest glanced at Patrick and smiled. "Troubled?"

"No," Patrick said. "I'm hoping I'm not messing up your schedule."

"Not at all," the priest said, shaking his head. "I'm on my way to see an old friend. Got the call last night that he was dying and wanted to see me."

"I'm sorry."

"No need," the priest waved. "He's a man who has lived a full life and has the scars to prove it. Some things you just can't fight and win."

Patrick frowned, remembering how his father had always said the exact same thing when he was younger. Every time luck turned on him, old man Lahm would shrug it off and recite the same phrase as if it were some kind of prayer. It was odd to hear it coming from the priest's lips.

"There's a motel a few miles down," the priest was saying. "I'm going to turn in there and wait until morning before going on my way. I'm sure you'll find what you need there."

Patrick nodded, trying to remember if he had seen the motel on his map earlier. They would definitely have a phone, and if there was no way to get moving before the morning, then at least he would have a bed to sleep in instead of the backseat of his car. Either way, it was a win.

"Lahm."

Patrick turned at the mention of his name.

The priest turned to Patrick and smiled. "See, I knew I recognized ya," he said. "Patrick Lahm. 'Faraway Places', I loved that book!"

Patrick smiled widely and sighed in relief, only now realizing that his heart had kicked into overdrive. He could feel a residual chill from hearing his name called out like that. It had sounded ominous in the otherwise quiet car.

"See, I told ya I might have read your work," the priest chuckled.

"I'm glad you liked it enough to remember who I was," Patrick replied.

"One of your best," the priest nodded. "I'm not much of a romance reader myself, but that definitely drew me in. You're one helluva writer!"

"Thank you," Patrick replied, easing into his seat as he pushed his laptop bag into the floorboard.

"Working on anything new?"

Patrick hated questions like that, and when he confronted eager fans who wanted any information on upcoming works, he usually handled things with a large dose of sarcasm. Answers varied from, 'Depends on what my editor forces me to do', to, 'Believe me, you'll be the first to know'. However, given the situation he was in and how much he currently depended on the man behind the wheel, he believed it best not to offend the priest.

"In and out of projects," Patrick lied. "The book signing has been taking most of my time."

The priest nodded. "It's always the little things that divert us from our true talents."

"Well, you could hardly call a book signing 'little things'," Patrick said. "It's important to meet the fans, shake hands, be an all-round nice guy. It's what gets the books off the shelves and the money into my pockets."

The priest glanced at Patrick, his smile barely moving, yet his eyes seemed to change. Patrick could almost sense a look of disapproval there, and wondered if the priest was judging him.

"Well, I'm just glad it's all working out okay."

Patrick watched the man for a few seconds before thanking him and gazing back out the window at the falling rain.

\*\*\*

By the time they had reached the motel, the skies had opened up completely and the rain was coming down in torrents. Thunder boomed in the distance between flashes of lightning that illuminated the skies for the briefest of moments before giving way to the darkness.

Patrick raced from the car and past the neon sign that welcomed its guests to the Kurtain Motel, followed closely by the priest as both men pushed into the front office. A woman and her son sat huddled on one of the couches in the corner, their bags damp with rain and their hair matted against their heads as Patrick quickly nodded a *hello* to them.

Neither returned the greeting.

Patrick took off his coat, folding it over one arm as the priest lightly tapped the bell on the front desk. They waited in silence, Patrick glancing back only once at the other two guests, until a burly man walked out from a back room. A cigarette hung loosely from his lips and his hair was combed back against his scalp, revealing bald spots. He looked at Patrick and the priest with little interest before pulling out a ledger and opening it to the date of the day.

"One room?" the man asked.

"Actually," Patrick said, interrupting before the priest could reply. "I only want to use the phone. My car broke down."

The man took a long drag from his cigarette before blowing smoke in Patrick's face. "Phones aren't working. The rain's ruined everything."

"Then do you have a cell phone I can use?"

The man shook his head and licked his lips, the pen in his hand poised over an empty space in the ledger as he waited to write Patrick's name in. Patrick sighed in frustration and looked at the priest in dismay. The priest shrugged and shook his head.

"Fine," Patrick gave in. "One night. Two rooms."

"Name?" the man asked, balancing his cigarette in the corner of his mouth.

"Patrick Lahm."

"And you?"

The priest was about to reply when Patrick stopped him. "I'm covering it. It's the least I can do."

The priest smiled at him and nodded.

Patrick looked back at the man behind the desk and pulled out his wallet. The man only grunted, taking another drag from his cigarette, and said, "Either way, I need his name."

"Harold Bell," the priest offered.

The man bent over the ledger, and Patrick looked back at the woman and her son. The boy was staring at Patrick, the look on his face deeply serious, and only smiled when Patrick waved at him. The mother, who seemed lost in her own thoughts, came to when she saw Patrick's gesture, and instinctively pulled her son closer. Patrick shrugged it off and turned back just as the man behind the desk set two keys in front of him.

"212 and 213," the man said between puffs of smoke. "Try not to break anything while you're in there."

Patrick gave him a half-smile. "Sure, we'll keep the partying to a minimal."

The man was not amused. "Cash or credit?"

Patrick took out his credit card.

\*\*\*

Owen Little watched as the two men walked out of the front office and skirted through the rain to the shelter of the motel canopy. He grunted and put out his cigarette, checking his log book as he counted down the names.

Seven guests tonight.

Owen smiled to himself. After weeks with only one guest propped up in room 215, things were slowly starting to look more promising. He reminded himself to pray to whichever god was responsible for tonight's downpour, and put the log book away as he glanced at the woman and her son.

"Lady, I don't think your cab is coming," Owen said. "You might as well just take a room and sleep the storm out."

The woman stared at him for a few seconds, not blinking, her brown hair falling in wet strands over her shoulders. She had come in less than an hour ago, claiming that a cab was on its way to pick her and her son up, and that she didn't want to wait in the rain. Owen had jumped at the opportunity to be in the company of a pretty face, but after a few attempts at flirting, it was apparent that she was not going to be much for conversation.

"Well?" Owen asked.

The poker face made him shudder. She was beautiful, he couldn't deny that, but there was something about her that just didn't sit well with him. He couldn't put his finger on it, but Owen knew trouble when he saw it, and this woman had trouble written all over her. If his wife were still alive, she would have probably set the woman up in a nice room free of charge and made her dinner as well. Owen was not his wife, though, and his instincts were telling him to send the woman packing.

"Lady, if you're not going to take a room, then you gotta get going," Owen said. "This isn't a shelter."

The woman blinked several times, as if waking up from a dream, and focused on Owen for the first time since she had walked in. She looked down at her son, patted him on the back and walked to Owen's desk, purse in her hand. She pulled out a credit card and handed it to him.

"In the morning, we can call you another cab," Owen said, turning his charm back on.

"That won't be necessary," the woman replied. "We can find our own way home."

Owen nodded and ran the card through his machine, noting the name Tara Frey at the bottom. "One night?" he asked, opening the log book again and writing in her name.

Tara nodded. "For now," she added in afterthought.

Owen reached for a key and handed it to her. "Room 214. Enjoy the night."

Tara looked at the key in her hands, rotating it between her fingers, then handed it back. "I would like a different room, please."

Owen frowned. "Is something wrong?"

"I'm a very private person, and I would like to stay away from the other guests."

Owen suddenly felt incredibly annoyed. "Listen, it's the only room we have. Take it or leave it."

Tara stared at him for a moment before saying, "You have seven guests here, and forty rooms. The one hundred's are closed off, I understand for renovation, but the others are all working. Rooms 219 and 220 are furthest from anyone."

Owen's eyes widened and his mouth opened and closed as he gazed at the woman with her outstretched hand, dangling the keys in front of him. "How do you know that?" he asked.

Tara gestured at the log book. "Guests and room numbers. All there."

*That doesn't explain how you know about the closed off rooms.*

Owen shrugged the thought aside and penned in Tara's name, handing over the key to room 219. She stared long and hard at it before tucking it away into her purse and gesturing for her son. The boy rushed to her, rolling the bags behind him with the ease of someone who was used to moving around with a suitcase.

"Thank you," Tara said, giving Owen a weak smile.

Owen watched the woman lead her son out into the rain as they trudged towards their room. He felt a chill race through him, and made up his mind that even if she asked, he would not extend her stay another night. In the morning, he would make sure both she and her son were gone.

## Chapter 2

Jason Collick stood motionless in his motel room.

His mouth was curled in a disapproving frown, and his eyes twitched as they darted back and forth between various corners of the room. He rubbed his hands together, feeling the uncomfortable sweat in his palms as he tried to control the shudders racing through his body. He had stood in the same position for almost an hour, bag resting gently against his leg, the suit he was wearing forcing beads of sweat down his nape and back.

*It's filthy.*

The single light above his head did little to hide what his eyes were quickly picking out. There, in a corner, a discarded napkin just below the left leg of the bed. Above it, a light stain that had not been properly washed out of the sheets, strategically tucked under the pillow to mask its presence. The small bathroom reeked of a mix of bleach and something a little more pungent, just below the surface, but enough to make his nose twitch.

He quickly reached into his suit pocket and pulled out a small bottle of hand sanitizer. He continued his scrutiny of the room as he squeezed the cold liquid into one hand and returned the bottle back into its designated place. He rubbed his hands together, squeezing the liquid in between his fingers as if this would somehow also clean the room around him.

*I can't sleep here.*

Jason took a step towards the bathroom and immediately recoiled when he saw the specks of dust bursting into the air around his foot, small particles that threatened to invade his lungs and clog his breathing. His frown deepened into a disapproving scowl. He took off his suit jacket and folded it carefully, placing it on top of his carry-on as he slowly undid the buttons of his cuffs and rolled up his sleeves.

He forced himself to cross the room and into the bathroom, quickly turning on the water. The faucet coughed sprouts of brown water, forcing Jason to gag, before a stream of clear liquid rushed out and into the porcelain sink. Jason covered his mouth with the back of his hand, closed his eyes and tried to stop himself from heaving. He took a few quick breaths before feeling his muscles relax a bit, and hurried back to his bag. In the outside pocket, he pulled out a small towel and returned to the bathroom, rinsing it out before using it to clean the faucet and sink.

Beads of sweat collected on his brow as he worked, his teeth clenched as he wiped off every surface of the bathroom, eyes watering at the strain caused by the fluorescents above his head. When he was finally done, he switched the lights off and sat down heavily on the edge of the small bathtub, breathing deeply, letting the surrounding darkness soothe him.

*You can't sleep in the bathroom. Get to work!*

Jason walked out of the bathroom and methodically began wiping down the small table and chair pushed up against the large motel room window. He had pulled down the drapes the minute he had walked in. He had wanted a room on the second floor, away from the prying eyes of the other guests. The man at the front desk – the disgusting man that smelt like cigarettes and alcohol – had told him that this was the only one available, and although Jason had accepted it, he wasn't happy.

*Just one night. You're only here for one night.*

Jason heaved his bag on top of the table, unzipped it and pulled out the spare sheets he kept for emergencies like these. In a side pocket, he grabbed a pair of surgical gloves. Within seconds, he had stripped the bed of the filth that had been covering it, and replaced it with his own sheets. He continued to work, wiping down the small commode and bedside table, and hesitating before deciding to clean the mirror as well.

A loud thump sounded from above, and Jason hissed at a cloud of dust that freed itself from the ceiling lamp as it began to sway gently. His eyes watched the small particles diffuse through the air, cursing as they slowly fell on top of the furniture he had just wiped clean. A second thump followed, and more dust blew out.

Jason fought the urge to race up to the second floor, kick down the door to the room above and throttle whoever was up there. His fists curled and he quickly closed his eyes and began counting to ten. He tried to control his breathing, and clenched his teeth tight when a third thump sounded.

*Happy place. Find the happy place.*

Suddenly, the darkness behind his lids gave way to a clear blue sky, cloudless and calm. Jason could feel the sand beneath his feet and hear the sound of crashing waves in the distance. A child was laughing somewhere in the background, and although Jason wanted to turn and see where the sound was coming from, he couldn't tear his eyes away from the clear blue above him. He instantly felt his muscles relax, and his breathing slowed to a gentle inhale and exhale that made him smile.

His therapist had walked him through this, taught him how to find the beach and clear skies whenever he felt that the world around him was too much to handle. Before that, he had taken his rage out on anyone or anything he could get a hold of; a lawsuit quickly waking him up to the fact that he did, indeed, need help. It had taken months to master the technique, to learn how to shut out each and every stimulus from the outside world. It had come in handy more times than none.

Jason opened his eyes. The thumping had stopped, and it didn't seem like there would be anymore. He sighed, allowing himself a quick smile before he remembered the dust and its deliberate dance through the air before settling on the surfaces around him. Jason clenched his fist, frowned and marched back to the bathroom to rinse his towel.

He was going to have to clean everything all over again.

***

Patrick Lahm felt a lot better as he stepped out from under the shower. Wiping the fog off the mirror, he quickly ran his fingers through his hair in an attempt to comb it into place. He immediately resented not going back for his bag when Harold had picked him up, right now wishing he had access to a clean towel and his brush. However, it was just for tonight, and the hot shower had done him some good anyway.

He walked out of the bathroom and frowned as he watched the rain falling outside. The storm was relentless, and he hated being stranded with no connection to the outside world. Still, he doubted there would be anyone out and about in this weather, and he felt a little safer about having had left his car behind.

He reached into his laptop bag and pulled out a charger, hooking it up to his cellphone and waiting a few minutes before switching it on. He lay back on the bed as the sing-song tone of the phone starting up filled the small room, and he sighed heavily when he noticed the absence of signal bars.

*Still no coverage.*

Patrick placed the phone on the bedside table and tried to forget about it, frustrated that he couldn't even reach his agent and let him know he would be late. A part of him had hoped there would be some way to postpone tomorrow's event, but apparently that was out of the question. He had been looking forward to this signing for months, his first tour since the trials. He would have laughed at the irony if his mood hadn't been so foul.

He sat up and reached for his laptop. Logging in, he clicked open a new document and gazed at the virtual white page in front of him. It was almost midnight, and despite the fact that he had wanted to wake up early the next morning and be on his way, he couldn't fight the urge to try and write. He silently hoped that maybe the weather could spark a little inspiration, that some good might come out of the situation he was in.

The cursor blinked in front of him, waiting, teasing, as if secretly knowing no matter how hard he tried, Patrick would not be able to write worth a damn tonight. Just like every other night. He bit his lower lip, calling on his mind to throw up anything he could use, some random idea he could just go with for a few pages to assure him he had not lost it completely. He was drawing blanks, though, and after a few more minutes of nothing, he was forced to admit failure and frustratingly slam the laptop shut.

He lay back down on the bed, noting the time on his cellphone and briskly looking at the empty bars before sighing and switching off the bedside lamp.

***

"It's good."

Patrick looked up at his editor and smiled. "Really?"

"Really," his editor nodded. "It's been a while, man, but looks like you finally came through."

Patrick's smile widened as he stood up and let out a long breath. He chuckled as his editor laughed along with him, tapping the manuscript sitting on the desk between them.

"Not sure about the title, though," his editor said. "A little too macabre for your readers."

Patrick waved. "Change it," he said quickly. "Do whatever you want with it."

His editor laughed and reached for his cigarettes. "Well done, buddy."

Patrick nodded and ran a hand through his hair. Seven months. It had taken him seven months to finally get the manuscript ready, his newest work after a four-year hiatus that left him dry and threatened to end his contract. He had sent it in with a heavy heart, unsure if it would be a good enough follow-up to his last bestseller, and had waited patiently for his editor to get back to him.

"This is very good news," Patrick said. He felt lighter, as if a weight had been lifted from his shoulders. "Real good news, man."

His editor nodded between puffs of smoke as he lazily flipped through the manuscript's pages. "Your style's changed a lot, though."

Patrick felt his muscles tighten. "Is that a good or bad thing?"

"It's definitely better," his editor smiled. "I just hope the fans appreciate it." He closed the manuscript and gazed up at Patrick. "Then again, I guess they'll just be happy you've released anything at all."

Patrick laughed and paced around the small office, shaking his legs and trying to work the knots out of his muscles. He hadn't known how stressed out he was until this very moment.

"When do we go into print?" Patrick asked, eager to get the process started.

"Well, there are a few edits that need to be tackled first, nothing too serious, and then we're good for business," his editor replied. "I'm thinking two weeks, depending on how fast you get the revisions done."

"Tonight," Patrick cut in. "You'll have all the revisions done tonight."

His editor laughed. "In a hurry, are we?"

Patrick smiled weakly. "I'm just happy it's done."

"Took a lot of effort, this one?"

Patrick puffed. "A whole lot of effort," he said. "Put my heart and soul into it."

His editor frowned. "Really?"

Patrick nodded.

"Funny," his editor said as he put out his cigarette and flipped through the manuscript again. "Seeing as you haven't written a single word of it, I find that hard to believe."

"Excuse me?" Patrick asked, his editor's words like a cold hand around his neck.

"You didn't write this, Patrick," his editor looked up at him. "You don't expect me to believe this is you, do you?"

"What are you talking about?"

"Oh, come on," his editor laughed and sat back in his chair. "You can fool the world, buddy, but not me!"

Patrick was about to say something when his editor stopped him. He watched the man reach out and rip off the cover page of the manuscript, then quickly circle Patrick's name below the title. He raised the sheet up for Patrick to see.

"Does this name deserve to be here?"

Patrick frowned in anger, unsure of how he was supposed to respond. His editor laughed and reached for the rest of the manuscript. Grabbing it in one hand, he bent over the small metal bin next to his desk, took out his lighter, and set the pages to flame.

"Hey!" Patrick shouted.

His editor dropped the manuscript into the bin and laughed again. "You're a fraud, Patrick," he said between chuckles, "and one day, you're going to have to confess to your sins."

"What?" Patrick asked, shaking his head in dismay as he reached for the metal bin.

The fires had died out, and just as he was about to reach inside to grab what was left of his story, the editor kicked the bin over. Patrick jumped back as millions of spiders crawled out of the bin, racing across the bright blue carpet of his editor's office, randomly scurrying in various directions. They were huge, the size of Patrick's palm, and of a dark black color that he was sure would have made them invisible if in a darker setting. Some made their way towards him, and he quickly stepped back and away, stepping on one that had been a bit faster than the others and had tried to crawl up his leg.

Patrick looked up at his editor in horror. "What is this?!" he screamed at him.

His editor was laughing. "Confess, Patrick," he cried out. "Confess and all will be forgiven!"

Patrick watched as the man threw his head back in merriment, his laugh almost manic as it echoed through the office. He was rocking right and left in his chair, his hands white as they gripped the sides while he swiveled.

Suddenly, the laughing stopped, and from the editor's open mouth, more spiders began to crawl out. Dozens of legs and bodies, one after the other, scurrying down the man's face and body as they raced to join their comrades.

"Confess," his editor gurgled.

Patrick raced for the door, wrestling with the knob as he tried to open it. It wouldn't open. Patrick looked over his shoulder as the arachnids grouped together and purposely moved towards him, a black carpet of moving legs that seemed to bulge and grow before him. Patrick stomped on a few more, but he was quickly overwhelmed by the sheer number of them as they raced into his pants and up his legs.

Patrick smacked at them, kicking out as he tried to rid himself of the millions of legs racing across his skin. But, there were too many, and in his panic, he toppled over and onto the floor. He screamed out in a mix of rage and terror, and through his open mouth, the first of many spiders crawled in.

## Chapter 3

Patrick sat up in bed, screaming out at the empty motel room.

The darkness was overbearing, and he quickly reached out and turned on the lamp beside him. In an instant, he was out of bed, smacking at his naked body, unable to shake off the feeling of tiny legs scurrying all over him.

He raced into the bathroom, quickly turning on the shower head and jumping under the water. He didn't bother with adjusting the temperatures, and immediately felt better once the cold water raced over him. He stood under the shower for a few more minutes, letting the aftereffects of the dream wash away as he tried to steady his breathing.

It felt so real, the meeting with his editor, the laughter still echoing in his head. It was as if he had actually been there, living it all. He felt a shudder race through him and he ran his hands across his body, trying to wash off the memory.

When he felt calmer, Patrick stepped out from under the water and gazed at himself in the mirror. His eyes grew wide as he noticed dozens of red spots across his torso, stretching from his neck down to his crotch and thighs. He ran a finger across one of the spots and winced in pain. He quickly made his way out of the bathroom and to the bed, squinting in the weak light as he checked for insects in the sheets.

The bed was clean.

Patrick reached for his clothes, scrutinizing the bite marks on his skin once more before pulling on his jeans and shirt. He grabbed his cell phone, noting the time and realizing that it hadn't changed since he had fallen asleep. The rain outside was still coming down strong, the night starless through the open window, and Patrick frowned in annoyance that he hadn't been able to sleep through it all.

*A drink. I need a drink.*

Pulling on his coat, he pocketed his cell phone and made for the door, looking over his shoulder once more at the bed and shaking off the residual feeling of spiders crawling across his skin. Once outside, the steady hammering of the rain calmed him down, and he smiled despite himself at the figure of Harold Bell leaning against the railing and smoking a cigarette.

"Couldn't sleep?" Harold asked between puffs.

Patrick shook his head and gestured to the cigarette, an eyebrow raised.

"A guilty pleasure," Harold smiled back. "I couldn't sleep either. Hoped the rain and a stick of cancer might do the trick."

"How about a drink?" Patrick asked.

Harold put out his cigarette, wiped his hand together and smiled widely. "You read my mind."

Patrick chuckled and threw an arm over the man's shoulder. "Just make sure you include me in your prayers, Father."

\*\*\*

Jimmy Frey watched the two men across the landing laugh and walk towards the stairwell. He didn't know them, but already made up his mind about how he felt towards each. He liked the taller one, the one with brown curls and the plaid shirt. He seemed like a reasonable man, one who would be able to see through the darkness and make sense of the confusion that was to come. He seemed like someone who could break free of the shackles that would imprison the rest of the guests here.

The priest, though. Well, that was a different story. Jimmy was immediately suspicious of the man, even in his holy attire, black hair combed back carefully and meticulously. When Jimmy had first stepped out of the room to enjoy the rain, the priest's figure had been shrouded in darkness, as if the holy man were a part of the night itself. Jimmy had shuddered just looking at the silhouette of the man, lighting his cigarette and leaning into the rain.

"You shouldn't be outside."

Jimmy turned to look at his mother standing in the open doorway to their room. Her eyes were sunken, and even in the scant light coming from behind her, she looked exhausted. He felt instantly sorry for her, wishing he could do anything to ease her pain, but knew that was beyond him. There was only so much he could do.

"Give me a minute," Jimmy replied, smiling at her.

Tara smiled back weakly and nodded, walking back inside but leaving the door open for him to follow.

Jimmy leaned over the railing and watched as the two men hurried through the rain, disappearing around the corner. He sighed heavily, gazing up at the sky as the rain splattered his face, and trudged back after his mother.

*\*\*\**

The Kurtain Motel was not known for being a homey place. People usually passed by the establishment without a second thought, quickly ignoring the welcome sign and opting to continue on their way rather than risk stopping. Almost in the middle of nowhere, at least ten miles away from the closest town. It sat eerily at the side of the highway, a beacon of dismay rather than hope.

What it had to offer was even less appealing.

The bar was a flimsy looking structure, nestled too close to the pool, its neon lights flickering on and off. It reminded Patrick of the old diner his mother used to work in, where he had been dragged to as a child almost every night to sit and color in one corner while she attended to a handful of guests. He immediately hated the damn thing, before even stepping in.

"As alluring as the motel itself," Harold said, voicing Patrick's thoughts.

Patrick nodded as they pushed through the door, immediately welcomed by a strong aroma of dampness and fried food. Patrick wrinkled his nose, making an effort not to gag. The bar was small, a few rickety tables strewn here and there coupled with stained, plastic chairs. Patrick noted an overweight woman sitting to one corner, three plates in front of her and a full mouth chewing slowly as she watched them enter. Patrick smiled at her, hoping he didn't look too uncomfortable and made his way to the bar with Harold close behind him.

"Didn't expect anyone out in this weather," the bartender grinned at them, placing two napkins in front of Patrick and Harold before going for one of the few bottles behind him. His hair fell in curls to his shoulders, and his goatee was as unkempt as the rest of him. To Patrick, it seemed like the man must have spent the night sleeping behind the bar.

"Get a lot of guests on normal days?" Patrick smirked, taking note of the name 'Connor' printed on the back of the bartender's shirt just below the Kurtain Motel logo.

"Depends on what you call normal," Connor chuckled. "The Kurtain isn't a popular stop anyway."

The man placed two glasses of whiskey in front of them and waited for their approval. Patrick raised his glass, took a sip and relaxed against the liquor's initial hit. "Good choice," he commented and glanced at Harold who was still eyeing the drink in front of him suspiciously.

"Want me to get you something else?" Connor asked Harold, who quickly looked up, smiled and shook his head.

"I'm quite fine," Harold chimed. "It's just funny how you guessed I would order this."

"Not a guess at all," Connor smiled. "It's all we have right now. That and water. We haven't restocked in a while."

Patrick laughed and downed the drink, pushing his glass forward and pointing at it for a refill as he winced. "Fill her up, buddy."

As he waited, Patrick glanced past Harold at the only other guest sitting at the bar beside them. With a baseball cap pulled down over his eyes, Patrick could barely make out the man's features, other than the athletic form of his upper body and arms as he cradled his own glass of whiskey. The man seemed almost embarrassed to be here, and Patrick wondered how many other guests in the motel had been stranded in this shithole because of the weather.

Not that Patrick could blame the man. From behind him, he could hear the mix of shuffling paper and chewing coming from the woman in the corner. The bar's foul aroma was slowly dissipating; either that or Patrick's nose was getting used to the stench. The lights were dimmed down in an attempt to make the atmosphere seem cozy, but all it did was add to the distaste Patrick felt towards it.

"So where were you off to before the storm hit?" Connor asked, placing the refill in front of Patrick.

"A book signing in Hartford," Patrick answered. "The good Father here picked me up when my car broke down."

Harold raised his own glass and smiled sheepishly.

"A night of celebrities," Connor whistled.

"Really?"

Connor nodded and leaned in closer. "Guy at the end of the bar, one with the cap?"

Patrick had half the mind to remark that the man was hard to miss, seeing as no one else was in the bar, but held it in. His ex-wife had always told him that his worst enemy was his own tongue, and Patrick was learning the hard way that she had had a point.

"What about him?" Harold asked.

"That's Cameron Turk," Connor whispered, his eyes wide as if he had just shared the most important secret in the world.

Harold frowned and shook his head, and Patrick was forced to smile. "Baseball, Father," he said. "The boy's a rising star in the Connecticut Tigers. They say he throws one hell of a curveball."

Connor nodded excitedly. "He's got talent, that one. Might even see him play for the Red Sox or Yankees one day."

"He's been absent for a few games, though," Patrick frowned, suddenly understanding the need for the pulled down cap and secrecy. "Some scandal about drugs?"

Connor scoffed. "Don't believe everything you hear on the news."

Patrick shrugged and took a sip from his drink, briefly looking over his shoulder at the woman busy licking the meat of her drumsticks. She looked up at him for the briefest of seconds before returning to her meal, obviously deciding her food was worth more attention than he was.

Patrick turned back and gestured to the woman with his head. "Is that our other celebrity?" he asked. "Pie-eating champion of the world?"

Connor gave him a disapproving loom before shaking his head. "Nah," he clicked his tongue. "The room across from here. Diana Bren."

"The actress?"

"Yup," Connor eased back into his child-like smile.

"What the hell's she doing out here?" Patrick shook his head incredulously. "She's a long way from LA."

"Heard she's shooting a new film up in Canada," Connor said. "Manager was telling me that she's booked herself the room for a week. Guess she isn't in much of a hurry."

Patrick had always enjoyed the romantic comedy flops that recently littered the young actress's career, an important part of his ritualistic mind-numbing routine at the end of slow writing days. And although he wasn't much of a baseball fan, he had been slightly interested in Cameron Turk's career, especially with the recent, drug-related rumors. Suddenly, the Kurtain Motel was starting to become a lot more interesting.

"You wouldn't happen to have a working cellphone, would you?" Harold suddenly asked, apparently bored with the celebrity chatter.

Connor shook his head. "Everything's down because of the rain," he said. "Television isn't working. Even my damn watch stopped ticking since midnight."

Harold nodded. "Mine, too," he mumbled.

Patrick took out his cellphone and noticed that it too had stopped at twelve am on the dot, and wondered if maybe he had actually slept a lot longer than he had initially assumed. The thought brought back images of his nightmare, and he quickly downed his drink in an attempt to wash the memories away.

Connor filled the glass up again.

*\*\**

Gina Andrews finished her last drumstick and looked up at the men at the bar just as they broke out into laughter. She felt her cheeks flush, the taste of hot sauce in her mouth mixed with a bitter taste of self-pity and paranoia.

*They're not laughing at you.*

She knew that. Of course she did. Still, it didn't help ease the tightness in her chest as she caught the man on the left quickly look at her before turning back to his friend and laugh. It felt like high school all over again, and she instantly dropped the drumstick in her hand onto her plate and wiped her mouth with the cuff of her sleeve.

She fought the urge to just get up and race back to her room, hide behind the closed door where she was safe and away from the scrutinizing eyes of strangers. She didn't have to escape anymore, she knew that. She had faced the laughs and jeers throughout her entire life, and she didn't have to do that anymore.

Gina had learned to focus her anger and push her bottled up emotions into her work, desperate to show the world that they were wrong about her. After she had made her first million, no one was laughing anymore. No, they were all polite and uneasy smiles, crawling around her and groveling for whatever scraps she would throw to them.

Yet, old habits die hard, and she sometimes felt like that seventeen year-old girl who had to hide behind the bleachers just so she could enjoy recess without being harassed. It didn't help that her small-town personality made her seem like a push-over, her girlish locks forcing people to treat her like a doormat until they realized who she was. She couldn't help being nice even in the face of sneers and ridiculous innuendos about her weight.

Watching the men at the bar laugh that way, so very similar to the laughs she had had to endure all her life, made her want to order another plate of drumsticks. Gina resisted, though; a small voice in the back of her head telling her that ordering more food would only make this feeling worse. She didn't want to have to look into the bartender's eyes as he brought her the food, his gaze reflecting what every man thought whenever they looked at her.

*Cute. If only she were thinner.*

Her cellphone suddenly rang, a shrill sound that echoed loud in the otherwise quiet bar. The men at the bar turned to look at her, and she felt her stomach clench with insecurity. She quickly reached for her phone and silenced it just as she noted her mother's number flashing on the screen. She swiped at the red decline button, unwilling to face another torrent of berating, and slid her phone back into her over-sized purse.

She looked up just as the taller man from the bar walked up to her table.

"Excuse the intrusion," Patrick said, flashing Gina a smile, "but is your phone working?"

*They always want something.*

Gina felt her fists clench and heat rise into her cheeks. She returned Patrick's smile as best she could and nodded.

"It's just that none of us have coverage," Patrick continued, gesturing towards his friend at the bar, "and I need to make an urgent call. Is it okay if I use your phone? I'm willing to reimburse you for the call."

Gina wanted to snap at him and tell him that she didn't need his money, but her instincts took over and her smile widened. "Of course," she said, handing him her cellphone.

Patrick thanked her and quickly dialed his agent's number, briefly noticing the logo on the phone's wallpaper. It looked oddly familiar, something he had seen on multiple occasions before, but he couldn't quite put his finger on it. He was about to ask Gina about it when he heard the monotonous beeping of a busy signal.

Patrick frowned in frustration and cursed when he saw the empty bars. He tried again, and when he got the same response, handed the phone politely back to Gina and smiled.

"I guess it's just my luck," Patrick said. "No bars."

Gina looked at her phone, confused when she saw that all four bars were full and that she had full coverage, and pocketed her phone. She was starting to feel very uncomfortable and wanted this small encounter to end as soon as possible.

"Sorry," Gina said. "Must be the weather."

"I guess so," Patrick said, smiling at Gina once more before returning to the bar.

Gina watched him walk away and let out a long sigh, her heart thumping in her chest. She quickly gestured to the bartender and reached for the menu.

She was suddenly very interested in dessert.

# Chapter 4

Diana Bren was furious.

The fact that filming had been postponed for a few weeks was one thing, but the fact that she was held up in this motel made her even angrier. She had immediately wanted to drive back home, give the producers the finger and tell them to find someone else as their leading lady. Yet, she knew she couldn't do that.

In the past three months, she had given up a lot of roles, taking her manager's advice and holding it for the big game. She was sick of her previous movies, films she knew meant nothing to the general public other than fluff. She didn't want to be the girl-next-door forever, and this particular opportunity promised to be a change from the usual. She would finally be able to show her true talents, prove to the world that she was more than just a pretty face.

Initially, she had been reluctant to film in Canada, her Arizona roots mixing well with California's weather. She had made a name for herself, albeit a small one, in Hollywood, and she knew that maintaining a lavish lifestyle in the midst of all the other stars was the only way to move up. Canada for six months meant missing out on some of the most important events of her career. Still, the movie was worth it, 'Oscar material' her manager had promised, and she had pushed her worries aside.

Now she was stuck in the middle of nowhere, stranded for a week in a shabby motel where no one would recognize her and she could wait for the call that they were ready for her. She had half a mind to sue them for her discomfort.

Diana looked out the motel room window at the rain outside and frowned. She hated the New England weather, a precursor of what to expect when she finally reached Canada. Not only was she immobile, she couldn't even enjoy the scant amenities the place provided. She eyed the pool longingly, raindrops forming dozens of ripples across the water's surface and blocking out the already dim lights.

She reached for her phone, looking to distract herself from her predicament and uneasiness, and tossed it angrily aside when she noticed the empty bars. She couldn't even escape online, and for a few seconds, the muscles in her body tensed in anger. She looked out at the pool again, weighing her options, and stood up in determination.

*Screw this.*

Diana opened her bag and pulled out her bikini. She vaguely remembered the man at the desk warning her about swimming in the pool at night, and decided that she didn't care. Besides, she rarely took advice from men who spent more time staring at her chest rather than her face. If she was going to be staying here for a week, she was damn well going to make the best out of it.

She stripped out of her clothes and pulled on the bikini, puffing as she tied the straps and adjusted the bra. If the little pervert was going to say anything to her about swimming at night, she was ready to give him a piece of her mind. Grabbing the room keys, she slipped into her flip-flops and stepped out into the night.

The rain seemed to pick up, and a short gust of wind sent shivers through her body. Diana hugged herself, as she looked out from the cover of the canopy into the night sky. For a split second, she wondered if maybe she was being a little too rash, that she would probably get pneumonia pulling off a stunt like this, but quickly pushed the thought away. If she hadn't taken risks, she probably would have still been in Arizona.

Diana stepped out into the rain, the cold drops making her flinch as she marched towards the pool. She glanced at the adjacent bar, secretly hoping no one would come out and try to stop her before she reached her destination. She rushed past the small gate, careful not to slip on the wet surface, kicked her flip-flops off and dove into the water.

The cold was refreshing, instantly hitting her and pushing away all her anger and frustration. She stayed under the surface, kicking her feet and propelling herself deeper into the center of the pool before finally surfacing. Smiling as she closed her eyes, she turned her face upwards into the falling rain and shifted her weight so she was floating lazily on the surface. Diana immediately felt a lot better.

\*\*\*

"What do you mean you *have* to go? You don't *have* to do anything!"

Diana stared at her boyfriend angrily. Three years and it was still as if he knew nothing about her. She crossed her arms and gazed at him impatiently, her open bag still half-packed with her plane ticket strewn on the bed beside it.

"This is a once in a lifetime opportunity, Jack," Diana said, her tone measured. "How do you not see that?"

Jack shook his head angrily and threw his hands in the air. "What the hell are you talking about?" he yelled.

Diana couldn't reply. She knew what she wanted to say, but it was clear anything that came out of her mouth would just go over his head. She hated Jack when he was like this, face all red, eyes popping out and the vein in the middle of his forehead pulsating. She could try to reason with him all she wanted, but in the end, he would only hear what he wanted to hear.

"You're throwing all of this away," he continued to yell, "over some role in a B-movie that nobody will ever hear of!"

"All of this?" Diana scoffed. "What exactly is *this*? What am I throwing away, in your opinion?"

"Our life!"

"What life?" Diana yelled. "You sell tires, I wait tables, and we can't even afford rent. Are you kidding me? What life?"

Jack stared at her in shock, his mouth opening and closing like a fish out of water.

"I've had it with *this life*, dammit!" Diana yelled, suddenly feeling a lot better now that her true feelings were out in the open. It felt relieving to finally let it all out. "I'm tired of waiting for someone to throw scraps at me just so I could get by. I have a chance to make something better of myself, and I'm not sitting back and watching it slip from my fingers."

Jack took a step back, shaking his head as he tried to register what he was hearing. Diana had never been open about how she truly felt about their living situation, a mutual agreement that had quickly spiraled out of control and had both of them staring into the abyss of life-long debt. He was clueless as to how bad things really were, oblivious to the bills and finances that he had quickly thrown into her lap to handle.

And now that she was pregnant, things would only get worse. Diana knew that for a fact, and was certain he would not see it that way. Which was why she hadn't told him about the baby yet, and had decided early on that she wouldn't.

"I'm going to LA, Jack," she finally said, her voice dropping to a reasonable level. "You're welcome to join me, but this isn't a negotiation."

She gazed back into his eyes, staring him down and waiting for a reply, unwilling to give in. When it was clear to him that she had made up her mind, he slammed his fist against the nearest wall and stormed out of the room.

Diana waited until she heard the front door slam before letting out a loud sigh and relaxing. She looked at her bag and ticket, shuffled her hair and continued to pack.

"You shouldn't be here."

Diana's head shot up at the sound of the strange voice cutting through the silent room. She looked around, clearly alone, and frowned in confusion.

"Lady, you shouldn't be here!"

\*\*\*

Diana's eyes flew open. She had drifted off in the water, and the hoarse sound of someone calling out to her had startled her. She kicked out instinctively, briefly swallowing cold pool water as she desperately tried to steady herself and stay afloat. She swam quickly to the edge of the pool, leaning out as she coughed and spat, gasping for breath.

The rain had stopped, and Diana shuddered at the crisp wind blowing against her wet skin. She looked over her shoulder, squinting at the silhouette of a man standing at the gate of the pool gazing at her intently.

"Can't you read?" the man sneered, pointing at a washed-out sign hanging to one side of the gate. Diana didn't have to make out the words to know what it probably said. She had, after all, been warned.

34

"Just wanted to take a swim," Diana called out, feeling a little uneasy at how she couldn't make out the man's features. She wondered if he was another guest at the motel.

"And that couldn't wait til the mornin'?" the man shot back. "I ain't gonna drag your ass outta that pool if you're found lying face down in the water. Get y'self outta there!"

Diana clenched her teeth, feeling the anger inside her well up. "How about you mind your own damn business and go find someone else to harass," she spat. "I'll use the pool whenever I frigging feel like it."

"Whenever I friggin–" the man mumbled under his breath, frantically opening the gate as he angrily stomped towards her. "I don't know who the hell you think y'are, lady, but this 'ere place got rules, and you'll follow 'em or find some other motel to haul up in where they don't care about corpses in their water!"

Diana didn't recognize the man. He stood tall, his long hair matted against his face and neck, looking ridiculous in his oversized pants and shirt. Against the pool lights, he shared an uncanny resemblance with the scarecrow at her father's farm, and Diana almost laughed at the comical scowl on his face. She was far too angry to be amused, though, and the fact that the man was challenging her only added fuel to the fire.

Diana pushed herself out of the pool and quickly stood up, staring into the man's wrinkled face and bracing herself against the strong stench of alcohol in his breath.

"I can buy this motel if I wanted to!" Diana hissed.

"And you can make the rules then," the man scowled, pointing a long, gnarled finger at her. "Until then, you's better follow the rules!"

Diana slapped the finger out of her face. "I can have your job over this."

"You go right ahead, lady," the man replied. "Tell Mr. Little that ol' Sal didn't let you swim in the pool after hours and we'll see what he'll say 'bout that." He smirked, and Diana fought the urge to slap the smile off his face.

"Fine," Diana pushed past the man, scrunching her nose against the smell emanating from his entirety and stormed away. "We'll see who'll be smiling once I'm done with you."

\*\*\*

"Confess!"

Jason Collick woke up with a start and he quickly pushed himself to a sitting position on the bed.

The room was dark, although he clearly remembered having had left a light on in the bathroom. He threw his legs over the side of the bed and felt around the cold floor for his slippers as he fumbled to turn on the lamp by his side. He found the knob, turned it and squinted against the sudden bright light.

"Confess!"

Jason's head turned to where he believed the voice was coming from, but he was alone in his room. He stood up slowly, a sudden throbbing in his temples forcing him to flinch and shut his eyes against the pain. There was a soft ringing in his ears that was slowly rising in intensity, as if someone were controlling a knob and turning up the volume.

"Confess!"

The voice was clear, even over the monotonous, ear-piercing sound inside his head. Jason raced for the bathroom, hands pressed against the sides of his head as his mind tried to determine what to deal with first, the pain or the inexplicable voice he was hearing in his empty room. The headache and ringing coupled together made it impossible for him to think straight, and he stabbed out against the medications he had lined up over the sink earlier on.

His eyes began to water as he desperately fumbled for the right bottle. When he found it, Jason quickly poured a pill out into one shaky hand and tossed it into his mouth. He didn't bother finding a cup, trained to swallow the pills without washing them down in case there was no clean water at hand. He staggered back against the bathroom wall and slid down to a sitting position as he waited for the effects of the pill to kick in.

When the ringing finally stopped, when the throbbing disappeared, he finally opened his eyes and took in a deep breath, letting it out slowly as he was instructed to do. Within minutes, he was calm again, and he pushed himself to his feet and walked out of the bathroom. He went straight for the door and stepped out into the cold night, taking in deep breaths, inhaling and exhaling slowly, allowing his senses to relax.

He looked out across the motel parking lot, bending his head from side to side as he massaged the nape of his neck. He heard shouting and turned to watch two people arguing at the pool, one of them breaking away angrily and storming off. He closed his eyes, letting the cool wind soothe him, still unable to shake off the feeling of dread that came with the voice he had heard inside his room.

Confess. Jason felt a shudder race through him.

"Quite a night."

Jason looked up. The old man leaning against the second floor railing was smiling down at him, a rolled-up cigarette in one hand as the other gave Jason a small wave.

"The rain brought a nice little breeze with it," the old man continued. "Cleaned the skies, too. You could see the stars all clear and bright up there."

Jason frowned. "Sure," he said.

"Name's Kurt," the old man said. "Nice to meet you. Didn't catch your name."

"Are you in the room above mine?" Jason asked.

Kurt Layton looked over his shoulder, then back down at Jason. "I guess so."

"I want you to stop whatever it is you're doing up there that's making all that noise," Jason said, his tone rising. "I can't sleep with all that crashing around."

Kurt shrugged and shook his head. "No crashing around up here," he said. "The arthritis keeps me pretty docile."

"Well, whatever it is you're doing, stop it," Jason said, "or I'll report you to the front desk."

Jason didn't wait for a reply and hurried back into his room.

## Chapter 5

Cameron Turk almost slammed into Diana just as he was rounding the corner on his way to his room.

He had spent most of the night drinking, already buzzed beyond what he considered acceptable, and had his cap drawn down low over his eyes. He wasn't looking up, careful to keep his eyes on the pavement as he tried to steady his gait.

The petite actress would have instantly caught his eye had he been paying better attention. Cameron had no idea who she was, but a dripping wet, bikini clad blonde was definitely on the top of his list when it came to flirt conquests. Tonight, though, he was in no shape or mood to turn on the Cameron charm and whisk the pretty lady away to his room.

Besides, it was important he keep a low profile.

Cameron had no idea whose idea it was that he stay hidden in this run-down motel, let alone how anyone had found it in the first place. All he knew was that, at the moment, it was best for him to stay away from the public eye until things at home had settled down. His manager had driven him out here personally, paid for two weeks in advance, and left with little more than a few warnings. He was to stay at the Kurtain Motel until they came for him.

It was probably one of the reasons his manager had taken his phone and left him without a car.

The first few days had been amiable enough. A working television kept him entertained for as long as he could stand reruns, and the front desk provided him with enough reading material to kill the long hours in between. When he was tired of both, there were always the pool and bar. Still, the days were getting to him, and all Cameron wanted to do was find someone to talk to.

He knew the bartender had recognized him, which really couldn't be helped. Cameron wasn't a celebrity, at least not yet, but the locals knew him well enough that the cap over his eyes would do little to mask his identity. Besides, how much of a threat could the bartender be? As long as Cameron made sure he didn't share too much information, then he was in the clear.

"Watch it!" Diana hissed, pushing Cameron to a side as she stormed past him.

Cameron watched the woman make for her room and smiled to himself. A part of him was already imagining himself with her as he eyed her slim profile, her long legs ending just before one of the most attractive behinds he had ever seen. He imagined pulling the strings of her bikini top and undressing her, his hands racing up and down her slender back.

*Snap out of it!*

Cameron shook his head and quickly pushed his fantasies to the back of his mind. He didn't need this right now. One of the main reasons he was here was to avoid temptation, the motel so far away from anything of interest that he would remain numb. He could already imagine his manager's disapproving look, scolding him and reminding him that this was not just a hideaway, but a form of rehab as well.

Cameron looked back at the blonde as she slammed her room door closed. He sniffed, pulling up the collar of his coat against the slight breeze and made his way to his own room. He would have to find some way to avoid her, although he doubted his capabilities in that. The light wasn't enough for him to get a good look at her, but what he had seen was enough to spark his interests, and that was never a good thing.

Cameron fumbled for his key and pushed into his room, carefully closing the door behind him in an attempt to prove to himself that he was more sober than drunk. He tossed his coat onto the chair by the window, stripped out of his pants and threw himself onto the bed. His head immediately began to spin and he felt his stomach turn. He quickly got up, steadying himself as his body began to sway dangerously, and took careful steps towards the bathroom.

The lights failed, Cameron's finger flicking the switch up and down to no avail. Deciding to rely on the light coming in from the room, he leaned against the sink's counter and turned the faucet.

The water that came out was thick, a dark brown color that looked uninviting in the dark. He bent lower, trying to take a closer look as he ran his hand under the liquid. It felt warm against his skin, and when he lifted his hand closer to the light, he realized that what he had mistaken for brown was a deep red.

"You killed me."

Cameron's head snapped up to his reflection in the mirror and his heart almost stopped.

Over his left shoulder was the reflection of a woman, her hair matted against her head, her eyes hollow and dead. She opened her mouth and the same dark liquid poured out of the dark abyss between her lips in torrents.

Cameron instinctively jumped out of the bathroom, hurling himself across the threshold into the light of the rest of the room, crawling away quickly as he turned to look over his shoulder.

The woman followed, slowly, her naked body stained with the blood oozing out of her mouth, her bare feet leaving maroon footprints on the carpet.

"You killed me," she said, her voice barely audible, a gurgle of words that he should not have understood. Yet, he heard her well, and he stared in horror as her eyes bore into his, dark and menacing, her fingers twitching by her side as she moved closer.

"Confess!" the woman hissed as she neared him, and Cameron quickly jumped to his feet. He was fully alert now, his stupor gone, and he raced for the door just as a hand grabbed him by the collar of his shirt.

"Confess!"

Cameron could feel her breath against his ear and he punched out blindly, throwing his elbows behind him as he tried to shake her off him. His swings connected with nothing but air, and Cameron suddenly found himself stumbling backwards onto the floor. He looked up hurriedly, trying to make out where his attacker was, his eyes darting back and forth across the room.

The woman was gone.

\*\*\*

"That's me for the night," Patrick said, slamming a hand down on the bar. He stood up and stretched, quickly noticing that only he and Harold remained in the bar. "Call it a night, Father?"

Harold smiled and raised his glass, only his second drink of the night in comparison to Patrick's five. "If my biological clock is right, it's almost dawn," he said. "I'll just wait it out. There's no sleeping for me now, anyway."

Patrick took a few bills out of his wallet and pushed them to Connor. "This should cover us both, buddy. Keep the change."

Connor smiled at him and nodded.

Patrick trudged out of the bar, tipsy and tired, already imagining himself lying face down in bed and sleeping like a log. He almost tripped on the two steps in front of the door and quickly steadied himself. The rain had stopped, and there was a slight chill in the air. He pulled on his jacket, dug his hands into the pockets and made his way to his room.

He turned the corner, watching his steps carefully, and began to climb the stairs when a shadow caught his eye and he looked up.

Jimmy Frey was sitting on the last step, arms around his knees and staring directly at him.

Patrick felt his weight shift, and he quickly grabbed onto the banister to stop his fall. He chuckled as he shook his head, his heart pounding in his chest.

"You scared the hell out of me, kid," Patrick said, looking up at the boy and wondering what he was doing sitting at the top of the stairs like that anyway.

Jimmy didn't reply. Patrick suddenly felt very uneasy; the way the boy stared at him was unnerving.

"Where's your mom?" Patrick asked.

Jimmy looked to his right, staring down the long hallway to the room he shared with his mother, then turned back to Patrick.

Patrick couldn't tell what was worse, how the boy was staring at him or the fact that he was sitting alone in the middle of the night. He looked barely over ten, and sitting there, completely still, reminded Patrick of one of those Japanese horror movies. He took a tentative step back.

"If you want, I can walk you back to your room," Patrick suggested.

Jimmy shook his head slowly. "You're needed down there," he said softly, his words barely audible.

Patrick frowned. "What do you mean?"

Jimmy cocked his head to a side, a gesture that scared Patrick even more than when he was sitting still. "He needs you," the boy said.

The door beside Patrick suddenly slammed open and Cameron Turk raced out into the night. Patrick jumped back, eyes wide as he watched Cameron stumble and fall. The baseball player scurried to his feet, racing forward only to stumble and fall again, this time rolling away.

"She's in there!" Cameron was screaming, looking over his shoulders as he tried to run away from whatever was inside his room. His eyes caught Patrick and he frantically waved at him. "Get away from there, man!"

Patrick shot a look back up at Jimmy, but the boy was gone.

Patrick staggered away from the stairs, his eyes set on the open door. He tried to make out what it was that was scaring Cameron, but he couldn't see a thing from where he stood. He ventured a few tentative steps towards the room, and stopped immediately when Cameron yelled at him.

"What the hell are you doing, man? Get away from there!"

Patrick looked at Cameron, then back at the room. His instincts were telling him to listen to the man, to get as far away from the room as possible, but his body had a mind of its own. He continued forward, stepping closer to the room and slowly stepping in.

The room was empty. The lights were a lot dimmer than in his room, but there was still enough light to assure him that there was no one inside. Patrick took another step forward, and his eyes immediately fell on the bloody footprints near the bathroom. He wondered if they belonged to Cameron; maybe the man had cut himself on a shard of glass inside, but the prints looked far too small. Patrick felt the same chill race through him, and he slowly backed out of the room, unwilling to investigate anymore.

A movement from the right caught his eye, and as he turned to see what it was, he froze.

From under the bed, a dozen black spiders scurried out. Patrick watched in horror as they came, spreading out across the room like a black rug, hundreds of them, thousands, a non-stop torrent escaping from the darkness beneath the bed. They moved around haphazardly, crawling over each other, racing across the furniture and covering everything in their wake. It was as if they were swallowing the entirety of the room as they moved, and still they came.

Patrick suddenly moved back, tripping over the threshold and falling down, arms flailing. He hit his head hard against the concrete, but the adrenaline kept him going, and he jumped up quickly. The spiders were racing towards the door, and Patrick raced forward, slamming the door shut and locking the arachnids inside.

He staggered back, putting as much distance between him and the room as possible, and only stopped when he bumped into Cameron.

"Did you see her?" Cameron stammered, hysterical. "She was right there, man. In the bathroom!"

Patrick shook his head, unable to make sense of what he had just witnessed. He had no idea what Cameron was talking about, but the spiders! It had been a nightmare. They weren't supposed to be in there. Nothing made sense, and Patrick quickly realized that he was losing his mind.

"She's in there, isn't she?" Cameron asked, holding onto Patrick's arm like a child grasping onto their parent. "She could come out, man. That door won't stop her."

"I didn't see anything," Patrick said, more to himself than to Cameron. His mind refused to believe what he had just seen.

"Man, are you blind?" Cameron yelled. "She was right there!"

"No one's there!" Patrick yelled, grabbing the man and shaking him. "The room's empty!"

"Then what the hell did you see?" Cameron spat. "What scared you so much?"

Patrick froze. He had no idea how to answer that. He glanced back at the bar, wondering if the commotion would have brought Harold and Connor out, but no one was running to their aid. Patrick's eyes darted across the other rooms, wondering why none of the other guests had come out to see what was happening.

He caught sight of a figure standing on the second floor, at the far end of the motel.

Jimmy Frey was leaning against the railing, watching them intently. If he had been affected by what was happening, it didn't show; he stood stoic and still in his place, arms crossed in front of him, and Patrick instantly heard his voice echo in his mind.

*He needs you.*

Patrick stared back at the boy, the uneasiness he had felt before instantly returning. It was as if Jimmy had known what would happen, as if he were waiting to see how things would transpire, a spectator to some freak show.

A few drops of rain startled Patrick, and suddenly the sky opened up and began to pour. The water instantly found its way into his coat, soaking the clothes beneath it, but his eyes never lost sight of the boy.

Through the torrents of rain, Patrick saw Jimmy nod at him and smile before pushing away from the railing and disappearing.

## Chapter 6

Owen Little hated athletes. And if there was one thing he hated more, it was being woken up by an athlete.

"I'm not staying in that room one more night," Cameron was shouting, pointing a finger at Owen and sneering at him.

Owen gazed at the man's finger and contemplated breaking it, clenching his teeth. He hadn't had a good night's sleep ever since his wife passed, tossing and turning in bed for hours until finally forced to give up completely and return to his post at the front desk. He hated the insomnia, and it made him edgy, all the time.

Tonight, though, he had fallen asleep almost immediately, and it agitated him that the much-needed rest had been interrupted by this raving lunatic.

Owen smacked his lips, reaching for his smokes and patting down an empty pocket. He cursed to himself, looking at Patrick angrily.

"What was wrong with it?" Owen asked, feeling like Lahm had a more sensible head on his shoulders.

"The room's haunted, man!" Cameron yelled. "Aren't you listening?"

Owen was listening, but nothing the jock said made any sense to him. Naked woman coughing up blood. It was ridiculous. He hadn't had a single incident in the motel since he and his wife had opened it up for business. If anything, it was more docile than the surrounding countryside let on.

Sometimes, Owen wished it were haunted. Sometimes, he hoped that someone would find a way to hang themselves in one of the rooms, or murder a prostitute, or maybe even an overdose of sorts. God knew the place needed a little spark. His wife had been against bad publicity, but Owen couldn't care less. Anything that brought crazy tourists and their money was fine by him.

However, Owen was far too tired to put his thinking cap on and try to find some way to benefit from what was happening right now. To have Cameron Turk say that the Kurtain Motel was haunted would have been a great opportunity to jump on any other night. Tonight, though,

Owen was close to slamming his fist in the man's face just to shut him up.

"I heard you the first time, Mr. Turk," Owen seethed. "I'm asking your friend here to shed some more light on the situation."

Patrick sighed, unable to fully comprehend what had happened, and unwilling to go into any details. All he wanted right now was for the night to be over so he could return to his car and get going. To him, this was all just a temporary hiccup, not a bit worth the trouble.

"Listen, you've got double rooms here, right?" Patrick asked.

Owen nodded.

"Great, just give me one of those and I could bunk with Cameron until the morning. Then you can change his room, or do whatever the hell you want."

Owen gazed at Patrick for a moment, then at Cameron. The jock was visibly shaken, his eyes darting back and forth as he constantly looked over his shoulder.

"It's more expensive than a single," he said, reluctantly pulling the log ledger out and setting it in front of him.

"I'm not asking for an upgrade," Patrick said. "Two singles for one double. If anything, you should owe me money."

Owen shook his head and gestured at Cameron. "His room's already paid for," he said. "We don't do refunds."

"Fine." Patrick took out his credit card and handed it to Owen.

"Is your room haunted, too," Owen smirked, jotting down Patrick's name in the ledger.

"Hey, man, this isn't a joke, okay?" Cameron shot.

"My room's fine," Patrick cut in, placing a hand on Cameron's shoulder to calm him down.

Owen glanced up at Cameron and his smile widened, clearly amused. "You're going to have to empty your rooms out."

"Little man, you need to listen," Cameron said through gritted teeth. "I'm not going anywhere near that room, not tonight, not ever."

Owen winked at Patrick, as if they were both in on the jest. "Was the woman a blonde or a brunette?" Owen asked. "That might help me understand better."

"You son of a–" Cameron launched himself at Owen, and Patrick hurriedly grabbed the man and pulled him away. Owen quickly staggered back, lifting his arms up and ready for a fight.

"Let go of me!" Owen forcefully pulled away and pushed Patrick aside. "Don't touch me!"

Patrick stepped up to Cameron, their faces so close he could smell the alcohol on the other man's breath. "Calm down," Patrick hissed. "I'm not exactly thrilled by this situation, but right now, I'm doing you a favor. I don't owe you anything. So, touch me again, and you're on your own."

Cameron stared back at Patrick, seething. "Whatever, man," he said, pushing past Patrick. "Just get the frigging keys."

Cameron stormed out of the small office, kicking at the small bench to one side before pacing back and forth angrily.

"Why are you putting up with him?" Owen asked, returning to the ledger. "You said it yourself, you don't owe him anything."

Patrick shook his head and waved a hand. He had already made up his mind about Owen, writing the man off as a bastard if ever he had met one, and he didn't feel the urge to let him in on anything. Besides, how was he going to explain that he was doing this because a little boy had told him to?

*He needs you.*

Patrick had no idea what that meant, but he was going to play along. He hadn't seen a dead woman in Cameron's room, but the spiders did not sit well with him. He tried to push the memory away, thinking that maybe he had just been hallucinating; a mix of alcohol and sleep deprivation. Yet, it didn't help him shake off the feeling of legs crawling all over him.

*Tonight. Just tonight, and then I'm gone.*

"Room 217," Owen said, handing over the key. "I'm serious about clearing out your rooms."

"I'll get my stuff," Patrick took the keys and turned to leave. "Cameron's room could wait until the morning."

"What the hell's *really* gotten the two of you so spooked?"

Patrick didn't answer, letting the door slam shut behind him.

***

Gina Andrews ignored her phone.

The ringing was getting to her, and every time she silenced it, the call would stop and start all over again. She stared in dismay at the caller ID before silencing the phone another time, and sliding it under the pillow.

The ringing started again.

Gina quickly got out of bed and paced her room. She had tried getting some work done to help her sleep, but for some reason, she just wasn't tired. Even the endless sheets of numbers, documents she regularly found a complete bore, couldn't do the trick. On the contrary, she seemed more alert than not.

She glanced at her watch and frowned when she realized the hands hadn't moved since the last time she had taken a look. She shook her hand, bringing the watch close to her ear, and let out an agitated sigh when she couldn't hear any ticking. She sat down heavily on the only chair in the room and gazed out the window.

Why wasn't she sleeping? On any regular day, she would be curled up in a fetus position, covers wrapped around her, sleeping soundly until the first rays of light woke her up. It made no sense.

The phone began to ring again.

Gina pressed her hands against her ears to stop the sound of the incessant ringing. She was in no mood to answer her mother now, nor was she in any state to listen to another lecture about her running away from her responsibilities.

She toyed with the idea of calling her lawyer and having him write up the paperwork her mother had been begging her to do for years. Gina could just hand over the entire company, and give the old woman what she wanted so she could finally leave her alone. It wasn't like Gina was emotionally involved anymore. She couldn't care less whether the company succeeded or failed.

What she really wanted was a break. A break from the responsibilities, the endless board meetings, the numbers, and most of all, a break from her mother. She had had it.

*That's not why you're running.*

No, it wasn't. Gina had to admit that to herself sooner or later, but right now was neither the time nor place for it. She needed to think, to get away and be with herself, and the Kurtain Motel was hardly the place for it. If it hadn't been for the storm, she would have driven through the night all the way to Providence. Maybe even Cape Cod. It didn't matter. As long as it was far away from Long Island.

The phone rang again, and Gina jumped to her feet and stormed to it. She grabbed it and swiped the 'decline' button. Staring at the phone, she waited to see what her mother would do now, hoping she would get the message.

When the phone didn't ring, Gina placed it down on the bed and sat back in her chair. If she couldn't sleep, then at least the rain would keep her company.

*** 

Jason Collick swallowed another pill.

The buzzing had started again, this time in the back of his head until it became a low drone. The headache was unbearable, ricocheting across his scalp as if trying to find one spot where it could hurt him the most.

Jason turned on the water in the shower, fell to his knees, and aimed the nozzle on his head. He grasped onto the side of the bathtub until his hands turned white, eyes squeezed shut as he waited for any change in the agony he was feeling. The pain wouldn't let up, and Jason found himself falling to one side on the bathroom floor, clutching his head as the pain soared through.

"Confess!"

Jason whimpered. He heard the voice, clear as day through the whirring and the pain, and he gently rocked on the tiled floor. There would be no rest tonight, he knew that. Although he needed the sleep, his meeting in the morning vital to the future of his company, it was obvious he would be spending the remainder of the night in his current position.

"Confess!"

"What do you want?" Jason screamed out, his voice echoing off the bathroom walls. He felt tears of pain build up behind his closed eyes.

The pain slowly started to subside, and he groped for the edge of the bathtub to pull himself to his knees. The buzzing continued, and although the sound irritated him greatly, he was grateful that it wouldn't be coupled with the headache any longer.

The thumping from upstairs started again, and Jason cursed out loud. He staggered out of the bathroom, reaching for his suit jacket as he considered making his way upstairs and giving the old man a piece of his mind.

Jason shook his head as the last remnant of the headache disappeared, and all he was left with was the drone of sound in his ears. He decided he would soldier through it, and with even more determination to pay the old man upstairs a visit, he reached for the doorknob.

"Pay your dues!"

Jason froze.

"Confess, Jason!"

Jason turned and gazed at the empty room. He was alone, yet the voice in his head was so clear, he could have sworn someone was standing right behind him.

"That was my daughter's college fund!"

Jason frowned, suddenly realizing that the buzzing in his ears was something else entirely. It was voices, hundreds of them, talking at once, whispering in his ear and echoing through his head. He couldn't make out what they were saying, but every now and then, one of them would be clear enough for him to understand.

"You took everything from me!"

Jason frowned, his hand frozen on the doorknob, his body suddenly very stiff. He strained to make out what the rest of the voices were saying, some of them almost familiar to him, yet he couldn't quite put a face to them. They were angry, threatening voices, and Jason could feel the chills race up and down his spine.

"I trusted you, you bastard!"

Jason flinched. The voices were obviously just in his head. He was being paranoid, the lack of sleep obviously getting the best of him. Yet, the words stung, and with every accusation he could make out, he felt as if he were being stabbed. He pushed away from the door and trudged into the center of the room, the voices inside his head suddenly increasing in intensity and volume.

"My entire pension!"

The headache suddenly returned, and Jason fell to his knees screaming. His hands immediately flew up and grasped his temples where he feared the pulsing blood would eventually force his veins to explode. The voices continued to come, some now more hysterical than others, and Jason could almost feel their hatred seep through him. He was engulfed by so much rage, his entire body seemed to be numb to anything else.

"Confess!"

Jason suddenly fell forward, the world around him darkening as he blacked out.

## Chapter 7

"This is typical!"

Patrick tossed his jacket on the couch and folded his arms across his chest. He had been dreading this since the moment he realized just how far past his deadline he really was. Although his editor was a flexible guy, he knew the publishers weren't. And it wasn't as if he hadn't been warned, several times.

Still, he had hoped he'd be done with his writing by now. Somewhere along the line, he had convinced himself that a few days of extra hours would help him achieve the desired word count. He was wrong, and the letter that his wife was waving around in the air was proof of that.

"I slave away, day in and day out, and all you have to do is sit at your desk and *write!*" Janine shouted. "A year, Patrick! A goddamn year!"

Patrick didn't need to read what was in the letter. He knew that the publishers had penalized his breech in deadline. He was a bit shaky on just how much the penalty was, but he was sure it was high enough to make Janine this angry. He couldn't bear to tell her that he wasn't even close to the required word count.

Actually, he hadn't written a word since his last book.

"For heaven's sake, Patrick, *I* could write a book in a year!"

"Then maybe they should have given you the contract," Patrick replied, a small smile escaping him.

Janine quickly crumbled up the letter and threw it at him. Their marriage was already on the rocks, one character flaw after the other suddenly getting on each other's nerves. After fifteen years and a son, they had just now realized that the small stuff did actually matter, and that the compromises each of them had made were too much to handle.

"Jokes! That's all I ever get from you!" Janine yelled.

Patrick was about to reply, but held back. He hated it when she got worked up like this, completely inconsolable and impossible to get through to. He had a hundred different excuses, things to say that would have gotten him out of this situation in the past, but he knew none of them would work. Not anymore. They were well past all that.

Besides, in hindsight, he couldn't lie to himself anymore. He knew that his reasoning would only shut her up temporarily and push the fight to another day. The truth was, he didn't have the energy to feed her lies and make up stories.

"Is Jack asleep?" he asked suddenly, his way of letting her know that he was not going to go through another night of yelling.

"We're not done here," Janine said through clenched teeth.

"Yes," Patrick said, walking away. "We are."

Janine stormed after him. "Patrick Lahm, I'm talking to you!"

Patrick turned around angrily, his eyes shooting daggers at his wife, a gaze that made her stop in her tracks and her eyes open wide. "Let it go," Patrick hissed.

Janine's eyes stared back at him in shock for only a second before her frown reappeared and she returned his threatening gaze with one of her own. "I'm not going to keep supporting this family while you sit at your desk and stare at your computer," she spat. "I'm not going to do it."

Patrick stared hard at her. "I said, let it go," he warned.

He didn't wait for her to reply, leaving her behind as he took the stairs by twos and made his way to his son's bedroom. He knew this wasn't going to end well, that in the morning they would definitely pick up where they left off, but for now, he just wanted to reassure himself that not everything in his life had gone to hell.

Jack was awake, covers drawn to his neck and eyes open, staring at the ceiling. He barely looked at his father as he walked in, and Patrick could see tears in the boy's eyes. He had obviously heard everything, but only today did Patrick see just how much the constant bickering was affecting his son.

"Hey, buddy," Patrick greeted softly, sitting down on the edge of the boy's bed.

"Hey, dad."

"You doing okay?"

Jack hesitated, his eyes staring at the ceiling. "I'm alright."

Patrick nodded solemnly, gazing about his son's room in an attempt to find something comforting to say.

"Are you getting fired?"

Patrick smiled. "No, kiddo, I'm not getting fired. Your mother just likes to make a scene out of the little stuff."

"It didn't sound little," Jack said, now looking straight at his father.

Patrick nodded and scratched the back of his head. "Yeah, well, we all have our ups and downs, buddy."

"Is it because you can't write anymore?"

Patrick shook his head and squeezed his son's hand. "I can write just fine. Hit a little speed bump, that's all."

"But doesn't that mean you'll lose your contract?"

Patrick hesitated. The thought had crossed his mind on more than one occasion, and he had desperately tried to push himself to write. The only problem was that nothing was coming out. The penalty was just the tip of the iceberg. Losing his contract meant starting from scratch, and it would be impossible to find another publisher once word got out that Patrick Lahm was all dried up.

"Don't worry about it. Your dad's always got a plan B."

"Why didn't you tell mom?"

Patrick frowned. "Tell her what?"

"About your plan B."

Patrick chuckled. He struggled to find a way to explain to his son just how complicated these things were. "It's not that simple, kiddo."

"Sure it is," Jack replied. "Just tell her about the guy who sent you his manuscript to read."

Patrick froze, his mind throwing up red flags as he fought to make sense of what his son was saying. He hadn't told anyone about that, and the only way Jack could have known was if he had been going through his computer.

"What manuscript?" Patrick asked, playing the fool, knowing that the only way to get any information out of Jack was to tread carefully, lest the boy realize he had done something wrong and bite his tongue.

"Your fan," Jack replied. "The guy you met at the bookstore, the one you gave your contact to when he told you about his book."

"How do you know about that?"

"Why didn't you tell mom that you read his book and you're going to steal it?"

Patrick felt the room suddenly go very cold. "What did you say?"

"The book," Jack replied. "The guy's book. Why didn't you tell mom you were going to send it to the publishers and say you wrote it?"

Patrick stood up quickly. "Jack, that's absurd. I would never do such a thing."

"Sure you would," Jack said, pushing himself up to a sitting position. "You're desperate. It's the only way."

Patrick looked back to see if his wife was nearby to hear this, then gazed back at his son in shock. Was the boy reading his mind?

"Buddy, that's stealing," Patrick said.

Jack nodded. "I know. It doesn't mean you won't do it."

"Of course I won't do it," Patrick almost yelled. "How do you even know about that? Have you been going through my computer?"

Jack smiled. "You can lie to yourself, if you want, but you can't lie to me."

Patrick took a step back from his son, his hands shaking slightly, his heart pounding in his chest.

"Confess, dad," Jack said, his voice changing, a much deeper, guttural sound. "Confess!"

Patrick watched in horror as the boy's mouth opened and dozens of black spiders began to crawl out.

\*\*\*

Patrick sat up in bed, sweaty and gasping for breath.

The television was still on, the program he had been watching long over and replaced by static. It was the only light in the room, and as Patrick tried to control his breathing, he looked around and noticed Cameron's empty bed.

He was alone.

Patrick threw off the covers and set his feet down on the cold floor. He could hear the rain outside, falling heavily, a brief burst of thunder in the distance and a flash of lightening close behind. His mouth was extremely dry, burning as if he had been screaming in his sleep. He quickly made his way into the bathroom, turned on the water and drank.

Patrick walked back into the room, switched on the small bedside lamp and turned off the television. He gazed out the large window at the night sky beyond and felt a shudder race through him. He glanced about the room quickly, half expecting the spiders of his dreams to come crawling out after him, but he saw nothing.

He couldn't shake off the dream. It felt too real, as if he had actually been living it, not just a spectator from afar. He remembered that night clearly, the fight with Janine that had finally led to the end of their marriage. Jack wasn't home that night. Janine had been careful to send him over to his friend's house so he wouldn't witness the argument. Patrick had to hand it to his ex-wife; she was good at keeping Jack away from their arguments.

*So why did it feel so real?*

Patrick felt the temperature in the room drop, and before he could dwell on the question for too long, he grabbed his coat and stepped out.

The cold hit him hard, and the wind forced the rain to slap against his face. He was alone on the second floor landing, not that it surprised him much. Only a fool would be out of his room in this weather, and he began to wonder what the hell Cameron Turk was thinking. He contemplated where the man could be, the only logical conclusion being the bar, but Patrick doubted it would be open at this hour.

Whatever *this* hour actually was.

Still no coverage or time orientation, and Patrick was beginning to feel that something was seriously off. He glanced to his right at the only room with a light on, two doors down, and guessed that it probably belonged to the boy from earlier. He considered knocking on his door, then decided not to. If there was one freak show cliché, it was a knocking at your door during a storm. Besides, the boy's mother would probably not take too lightly to a complete stranger drenched in rain asking to speak to her son.

Patrick pulled up his coat collar, braced himself and turned left, walking down the landing to his previous room and Harold's. If the priest was awake, it would provide some relief from how Patrick was feeling right now. The emotions he had felt in his dream still lingered, and try as he would, he just couldn't rid himself of the feelings of shock and terror that were coursing through him.

He rarely thought about his family these days. After their divorce, he and Janine had gone their separate ways. The custody battle had been horrendous, but Patrick had admitted to himself early on that his son was probably better off with his mother than with him. There wasn't much he could offer the boy anyway, and without Janine's support, Patrick had been forced to sell almost everything he owned until his last book came through.

But eventually, it had come through. And it hit number one within weeks.

Patrick remembered a time when he had wanted to call Janine up and throw it all in her face, a childish perversion to prove he was still better than her. The feeling had passed pretty quickly, though, especially when his editor had called and told him that he was being sued by an angry fan.

Patrick shook his head in anger as he recalled the four month trial and the endless inquiries he had had to endure. At that time, he had been happy that Jack wasn't around to witness it all, although the ordeal had quickly become a national interest. At one point, Patrick couldn't walk around downtown without someone stopping and harassing him.

Room 213 was hidden by the canopy's shadows, but the rain still found a way to break through the cover. It made a continuous tapping sound, as if someone were impatiently drumming their fingers against the window and door. Patrick couldn't see any light on, and despite the immediate reluctance to wake the priest, he knocked on the door.

Patrick waited, glancing at his previous room while he buried his hands in his pockets. He had emptied it out as promised, looking over his shoulder at the bathroom every few seconds, hoping that Cameron's ghost was confined to the room downstairs. He had felt foolish, but after what he had seen, he wasn't going to leave anything to chance or logic. He was on an emotional cruise control as his brain sat on the sideline with hotdogs and chips, watching the events of the night unfold.

Patrick knocked again, and when there was still no answer, he cupped his hands over his eyes and peered into the room through the window. The rainwater made things far too blurry, but Patrick could tell that the room was empty. Thunder burst behind him and made him jump, the following flash of lightning momentarily illuminating the motel and confirming its emptiness.

Patrick frowned and walked towards the stairs, grasping the banister tight as he descended, careful not to slip on the water that raced down ahead of him. At the bottom, he glanced around the corner and saw that the bar's neon lights were off and the windows dark. He turned to his right, quickening his step as he passed Room 203, Cameron's room, hoping to God that the man had not changed his mind and decided to return to it in the middle of the night. A television was on in the next room, the soft white light of static flickering through the window. From the corner of his eye, Patrick could see a figure sitting beside the window, and he briefly wondered how anyone could fall asleep on that uncomfortable chair.

Patrick dug his hands deeper into his pockets and hunched his shoulders, the rain seeping in through the collar of his coat down his nape. He continued to the front office where a light was on inside, and hoped that Harold had decided to have another cigarette in the comfort of the fluorescents with a magazine to kill the time. He doubted that the priest had found a way to fall asleep, either, and right now, Patrick needed the company.

The office was empty.

Patrick stomped his feet on the welcome rug just inside the door and glanced about the small space in dismay. He walked up to the front desk, rang the bell and waited, looking out longingly at the highway beyond. He remembered his car and hoped that, come the morning, he would find it waiting for him by the side of the road where he had left it. Right now, he would have done anything to be on the open road, driving towards Hartford, even in the storm. Anything was better than this.

When no one came out, Patrick rang the bell again and glanced into the small backroom. When he had come in earlier with Cameron, Owen had been sleeping on a chair inside, but the room was empty now. Patrick sighed and ran a hand across his face, yawning. He was exhausted, yet unwilling to venture back into the world of dreams. He needed something to get his mind off of his recent nightmares. Maybe he could find where Connor was staying and convince the big man to open the bar for another hour.

*The world doesn't revolve around you, asshole.*

The voice in his head sounded too much like Janine for comfort.

Patrick glanced back out at the rain, contemplating returning to his room and trying to sleep, but couldn't bring himself to move. He was reluctant to return to the cold and rain, but there was nothing in here that spiked his interest, and the couches looked too uncomfortable to lay back on should he decide to sleep.

Movement from across the motel caught his eye, and he squinted to get a better look at the figure racing under the canopy and around the corner. It looked like a woman, but Patrick couldn't tell for sure. She seemed to be heading towards the bar.

Patrick stepped out into the rain and made his way in her direction. She was bound to turn back once she noticed the bar was empty, and he hoped to run into her on her return. Right now, he would settle for anyone to talk to, provided he didn't scare her half to death.

"Where are you going?"

Patrick jumped, feeling his heart leap into his throat. He glanced to his left at the small figure of Jimmy Frey standing completely still in the rain, hair soaked and almost covering his eyes, water streaming down his face. He was dressed in a Simpsons shirt and shorts, both fabrics looking far too flimsy for this weather, yet he seemed unaffected by neither the cold nor the rain.

"Kid, what the hell are you doing out here?" Patrick asked, his brain screaming at him to pull the boy out of the rain, yet his instincts telling him otherwise. Patrick couldn't explain it, but he had a feeling that being too close to Jimmy would not be in his best interest.

"I saw you from my room," Jimmy replied. "I thought you might be looking for something and needed help."

Patrick smiled despite himself. "That's sweet, kid, but you really shouldn't be out here in the rain like this. Your mother's going to have a fit."

Jimmy shrugged and smiled, and for the first time, Patrick could sense there was a human being inside the little boy's body. "Mom's busy."

Patrick gestured towards the end of the motel. "Was that her running off that way?"

Jimmy kept his gaze set on Patrick and nodded.

"What's she doing over there?" Patrick asked, venturing a few steps towards the boy. "The bar's closed."

"She doesn't drink," Jimmy said.

"What then?"

"She didn't say."

Patrick stared at the boy for a moment, only then realizing that they were still standing out in the open.

*The kid's going to get pneumonia,* he thought to himself.

Still, he hesitated. He would have expected Jimmy's small frame to be shaking in this weather, yet there was no sign that the boy was in any way uncomfortable. On the contrary; he seemed extremely content standing just where he was.

"You sure you're okay out here?" Patrick asked, hoping to remind the boy that there was nothing ordinary about him being out in a storm dressed the way he was.

Jimmy only nodded, and Patrick was forced to smile. He remembered how his own son always tried to feign being okay even when he wasn't.

"What's your name, kid?" Patrick asked.

"Jimmy."

"Well, it's nice to meet you, Jimmy," Patrick smiled. "I'm Patrick."

Jimmy nodded, and Patrick could sense that it was more of a confirmation nod than anything else, as if the boy had already known.

"What do you say we step out of this rain?" Patrick asked. "I'll walk you to your room and you can change into something less wet."

"That's okay," Jimmy said. "Most of this isn't real anyway. I'm not really wet."

Patrick frowned. "What? What do you mean?"

Jimmy shrugged and smiled again. "It's complicated."

Patrick was a little amused at the game Jimmy was playing, impressed by how the imagination of the young mind could make anything seem 'complicated'. He walked towards the boy and reached out a hand.

"Humor me, then," Patrick said with a smile.

Jimmy grasped his hand, and for a brief second, Patrick felt a shock of electricity race through him. It was short and strong, and it almost threw him back. He looked down at the boy and smiled through the numbness, trying to feign easiness as they walked back under the safety of the canopy.

"Hey, Jimmy, can I ask you something?"

Jimmy nodded as they began their ascent to the second floor.

"It's about what you said earlier," Patrick said. "Remember when we first talked? You were on the stairs over there."

Jimmy nodded again, looking up at Patrick patiently.

"How did you know about Cameron?" Patrick asked. "You said I was needed."

Jimmy shrugged. "You were, weren't you?"

Patrick gave the boy a half-smile. "In a way, I guess I was." They stopped at Jimmy's room and looked at each other. "But how did you know?"

"I guess I just knew."

"Are you psychic, kid?"

Jimmy frowned. "What do you mean?"

"Never mind," Patrick said, waving it off as the boy opened the door to his room and stepped inside.

Jimmy stopped and turned back to Patrick. "The bar isn't closed," he said.

"Sure it is," Patrick said. "I just checked."

"You were checking somewhere else," Jimmy said, pointing past Patrick. "Now everything's different."

Patrick turned around to see what the boy was pointing at, and noticed that it had stopped raining. Not only that, but as he bent over the inexplicably dry railing and looked down, it was as if it hadn't been raining at all. The entire parking lot was dry, his clothes were dry, and even the wind had let down tremendously, making Patrick feel a little too warm in his coat.

"Long night, eh?"

Patrick turned to see Kurt Layton leaning against the railing with a cigarette in his hand, a wide smile on his face. He was clad in just his boxers with an open robe thrown over his shoulders.

Patrick turned to Jimmy, but the boy had gone into his room and closed the door.

"Quiet, that one," Kurt said. "His mother's quite a looker."

Patrick looked at the old man and shook his head in bewilderment. Now he really needed a drink.

## Chapter 8

"How much?"

Kurt Layton finished rolling his cigarette, slowly, taking his time as he pretended to run the numbers through his head.

He already knew what he was going to charge, but when it came to Ivy League medical students, he found that it was important to look like he was putting in more effort than he really was. He had quickly learned that in his profession, and any other profession he had ever worked in, the more it seemed like a hassle to finish a job, the more people were willing to pay. And Kurt loved money.

"A grand," he finally said, sticking the cigarette in his mouth and lighting it.

The undergrad's eyes flew open. "That's a little steep."

"You think?" Kurt asked. "Well, if you feel that strongly about it." Kurt stood up and adjusted his coat. "Thanks for the coffee."

"Wait, wait, just sit down," the undergrad said.

Kurt smiled to himself. He could smell desperation from a mile away, and the kid in front of him reeked of it. He immediately knew there would be no need for negotiations.

"How long?" the undergrad asked.

Kurt shrugged and sat back, locking his palms together behind his head as he stared at the ceiling. The truth was, he already had the bones at home. He never left things to chance, digging up whatever he could whenever the opportunity presented itself. It was a risky business, and he never left things to chance.

"A week, maybe two," Kurt replied, looking back at the young man. "You in a hurry?"

"Of course I am," the undergrad replied. "I've got finals in a month."

Kurt leaned forward and blew smoke out of his mouth in rings. "I could push the schedule, but that will cost you an extra three grand."

"Forget it!"

Kurt shrugged and made to get up again before the young man grasped his arm. Kurt raised an eyebrow at him and settled back into his seat.

The undergrad sighed and shifted in his seat, looking about the small diner restlessly. It was more money than he had anticipated, and Kurt believed that the kid would go through hell trying to explain it to his father. He couldn't care less, though. All Kurt cared about was getting paid, and he rarely lost sleep over how anyone he did business with went through to fulfill that.

"Make up your mind, son," Kurt said. "I have appointments to keep."

The undergrad looked at Kurt angrily, then sighed and nodded. "How do I pay you?"

Kurt smiled. Now they were getting somewhere.

***

The baby was crying again.

Diana opened her eyes and let out an agitated sigh. She had first heard the screaming when she returned from the pool, angry and frustrated. She had been ready to raise hell, changing quickly as she ran the words she had wanted to say through her head. She had made up her mind. Diana would get the old man fired, wait until the morning, then take her deposit and find another motel. She didn't need to put up with this crap.

That was when the crying had started. It startled Diana, forcing her to pause in mid-dress while she tried to make out where the sound was coming from. At first, it had sounded like it was in her room, but she knew better and assumed it was either the woman in the room around the corner, or some new guest stupid enough to take their baby out in the rain.

It had quieted down soon enough, but not before it took the fight out of Diana and had her give up on the idea of complaining. She had undressed grudgingly and crawled under the covers, resolving to wait until the morning and decide then whether or not to continue with her plan. A part of her knew that it wasn't worth the trouble, but a bigger part wished for nothing else than to see *Ol' Sal* squirm at her feet and beg her not to get him fired. That grin on his face had been the worst of it, the smug look of someone who truly believed she wouldn't be able to do anything to him.

She'd show that arrogant prick who Diana Bren really was. She had fallen asleep with a slight smile on her face as she imagined all the things she would do to make the man suffer.

That's why she was less than happy when the crying started again.

Diana sat up in bed, reaching for her bra and snapping it on as she rolled to her feet. She pulled on her shirt and grabbed her phone to check the time. It was still midnight, and she frowned, thinking that maybe there was something wrong with her phone. She remembered it had been twelve when she had gone to bed. She caught sight of the empty signal bars and quickly tossed the phone aside, useless.

When the crying grew louder, Diana grabbed her jeans and started to pull them on. This time it felt a lot more like the baby was actually in her room, and Diana frowned in confusion. She didn't believe the walls could be so thin. She had deliberately chosen her room because there were no rooms above her, and the one next to hers was being renovated.

*The crying shouldn't be this loud!*

She glanced around the room again, trying to reassure herself that she was alone, and that there was no way a baby could be hiding in some corner without her knowing about it. Still, the wailing was much too loud for comfort, and Diana cringed at the sound.

*Somebody shut it up!*

She had to get out of here. Pulling the door open, she froze in horror when her eyes fell on the baby sitting right outside her room. It looked up at her, naked, eyes strung with tears, mouth wide open as it screamed. There was blood streaming down the side of its face from a large scar on its head, and Diana's first thought was how it was alive to start with. She staggered back, her hand on her mouth as she stared at it.

The baby continued to cry, its eyes on Diana as she backed away. As if sensing it would be left alone, it rolled onto its hands and knees and crawled towards her, wailing as blood splattered around it. It quickened its pace, blind to anything except Diana as it made its way straight for her.

The bed threatened to stop Diana's retreat, but she quickly climbed on top of it and kicked her way to the far wall. The baby stopped its advance a few feet away from her. It had stopped crying, and Diana couldn't pull her eyes away from the pulsating scar on its head.

It looked up at her, sniffing, eyes watery.

"Confess!"

Diana couldn't tell whether the voice came from the baby itself or from somewhere else, but it chilled her to the bones. She couldn't tear her eyes away from the baby, watching as the blood slowly began to fall down into its eyes and mouth.

"Confess!"

This time Diana was sure where the voice had come from, the baby's mouth moving. She stared in horror as its lips curled into a smile, blood dripping down its chin and onto the carpet.

When it began to crawl towards the bed again, Diana screamed.

*** 

"It's a long night, that's for sure," Kurt Layton said.

Patrick walked beside the old man quietly as they made their way to the bar, declining a rolled up cigarette and only stopping once as Kurt cupped his hands to light his own.

"I usually sleep through the night," Kurt was saying. "Never really noticed how it lingered. Not like the day, mind you. During the day, there's a lot to do, you never really take notice of the time. But at night, it's just you and the dark."

Patrick nodded, not really paying much attention to the old man's words. He was still a little shaken, unsure as to how he should feel about the past few hours. Nothing about tonight made any sense, and it was hard to keep pinning things on the drinking and sleep deprivation.

"You okay there, son?"

Patrick looked up at Kurt and smiled. "Sure," he lied. "Like you said, long night. A drink could do me well."

"Amen to that!" Kurt chuckled as they continued on their way.

The screaming startled them, and it only took a few seconds for the two men to look at each other before racing towards the sound. The screams grew louder as they rounded the corner, and from the corner of his eyes, Patrick could see that the bar actually was still open, its neon sign flickering in welcome.

Kurt wrestled with the knob to room 202-B, pushing against the frame as he tried to wrestle the door open. The screaming inside continued, shrill and piercing, and Patrick could have sworn he heard the sound of a crying baby beneath it. He glanced back at the bar just as Cameron and Harold came running out, followed closely by Connor.

"Kick it open!" Patrick yelled, the woman's screams like knives in his head. He could almost feel her fear like a cold hand squeezing on his heart. From around the corner came the sound of another room's door opening, and in seconds, the overweight redhead from the bar earlier came rushing to them.

"What's going on?" she yelled over the screaming.

Kurt threw his weight against the door and stepped back, wincing in pain as he grabbed his shoulder. Patrick pushed him aside, took a few steps back and then charged at the door. He slammed his foot down on the knob, jolts of pain bursting up his leg as he heard the satisfactory breaking of wood. The door swung open forcefully and slammed against the wall. Patrick staggered and almost fell if not for Harold grabbing him by the arm and steadying him. Kurt and Gina raced into the room.

\*\*\*

"Drinks on the house for the knights in shining armor."

Connor sat two glasses of whiskey in front of Patrick and Kurt, smiling uncomfortably.

"Thanks, Connor," Kurt said, getting up and walking over to a table nearby.

Patrick downed his entire glass without a word. He looked over at where the blonde actress sat, visibly shaken as Gina Andrews tried to comfort her. He couldn't get the screaming out of his head, Diana's shrill cries resonating in his mind and scraping at the inside of his skull. If she had been screaming right in his ear, it wouldn't have affected him the same way. No, it was almost like he had been in her head, experiencing her fear, going through the same hell she had gone through.

Patrick felt a hand rest on his shoulder and squeeze. He turned to look into the tired eyes of Harold Bell.

"You seem to be tonight's protagonist," Harold said.

Patrick sniffed and shrugged. "It's a strange night."

"Doesn't take away from the fact that whatever had scared that poor girl, she was lucky you and Kurt were there to help."

Patrick didn't reply, tapping his glass for a refill, his eyes fixated on Diana. The woman was pale as a sheet, and her eyes kept darting back and forth in search of some inexplicable wraith. He couldn't tell for sure what she had seen, the image of her cowering on her bed still fresh in his mind, but he had a pretty good idea what it might be.

He couldn't deny it anymore. He began to believe that maybe there was some truth to what Cameron had said earlier, that maybe the motel really was haunted. How else could he explain what was happening to the guests, or to him for that matter? There was something strange going on, and the more Patrick dwelled on it, the more it hurt his head.

Then, of course, there was his last encounter with Jimmy. The rain that never was, the conversation that had probably never happened. There were too many questions rolling about in his head, and he was nowhere close to answering any of them. He gazed about the bar, at the guests who had made their way inside and were scattered all around. He saw the way Cameron was looking at the actress, an understanding in his eyes as if knowing how she felt. He saw Kurt's faraway stare and could almost hear his mind at work. He saw Connor wiping down the bar, the circular motion set in the same spot as if he were working on cruise control.

Everyone could sense it, in one way or another. And Patrick hated that no one had a clear explanation.

"Is your watch working?" he asked Harold.

Harold shook his head. "Still at twelve."

"Does it feel like time isn't passing?" Patrick frowned. "It's been dark for far too long. Shouldn't we be seeing dawn by now?"

Harold shrugged and pulled himself up onto a stool. "It's a little strange, but then again, the night has a way of dragging out."

Patrick clicked his tongue. "Seems like it's taking its sweet time."

"Are you scared of the dark?" Harold chuckled, taking a sip from his drink.

"I'm scared of the lack of sleep," Patrick answered, shrugging off his worries for the time being. "I'm not going to be in any form to drive tomorrow morning if I don't get some proper rest."

"I feel the same way," Harold said, "although a while ago, I was sure I could make it to dawn alright."

Patrick nodded. He had half expected to see the first signs of sunrise by now, an indicator that the wait was over and he could finally get back on the road. Plus, he'd had enough excitement for one night, and the only thing stopping him from going back to his room and trying to sleep was the fear that he would be plagued with more nightmares.

"Did she say anything to anyone?" Patrick asked.

Harold shook his head. "I'll be honest, though, I haven't asked."

Patrick frowned. "God, her screams, father," he said. "It was like she was screaming in my head."

"I can imagine," Harold replied. "We heard them all the way in here. I could have sworn the glass shook."

"What could scare someone like that?"

"Ghosts, man," Cameron said as he idled towards them, setting his drink on the bar next to Patrick's and leaning over it. "After what I saw, I'm not surprised."

Harold leaned over and gazed at Cameron with a childish look of curiosity. "What did you see?"

"A woman," Cameron said. "Someone I once knew. Dead. She came at me in the bathroom, man, and I swear, it was like she had crawled out of her grave. Scared the bejesus out of me." Cameron glanced at Patrick. "This guy says he saw nothing, but I don't believe it one bit. He was shitting coins when he went into my room."

Harold raised an eyebrow and looked at Patrick in amusement. "You saw her?"

Patrick shook his head. "I didn't see a woman," he said.

"Bullshit!" Cameron scoffed.

Patrick gave him a disapproving look, then turned his attention back to the women at the table. Gina put a hand on Diana's shoulder and the actress flinched.

"I saw something, but not a woman," Patrick finally said, taking a sip from his drink.

Cameron was suddenly interested, standing up and gazing at Patrick as he waited for him to continue. Patrick gave him a quick look and shook his head.

"Doesn't matter," Patrick said. "I was tipsy. Probably imagined it all."

"What was it?" Cameron asked.

Patrick hesitated before finally saying, "Spiders."

"You saw a spider?" Harold asked, the tone of his voice a little skeptical.

"Not one spider, father," Patrick said. "Hundreds of them. Crawling out from under the bed. They were coming for me."

Harold shook his head in bewilderment. "That is quite strange."

"Why would you see spiders?" Cameron asked. "Are you scared of them or something?"

"Why did you see a dead woman?" Patrick asked.

Cameron stared at Patrick a moment longer before grabbing his drink. "Whatever, man," he said and walked away.

Patrick watched him leave and turned back to Diana. She was looking at him now, her eyes boring into his. He couldn't read minds, but he knew exactly what she was thinking. Whatever was happening at the Kurtain Motel, it wasn't going to leave anyone out.

## Chapter 9

Jimmy Frey sat silently in the chair next to the window. He gazed out into the night, sighing heavily when he began to notice the few droplets of rain falling on the railing outside. It was starting again, and he was too tired to keep up.

He glanced over his shoulder at his mother as she sat motionless on her bed, eyes closed, meditating. He wondered if she would have the energy to go through another round, especially after the last one had almost drained her completely. She wouldn't complain, he knew that. She was strong, and he admired that about her. Still, he worried.

Jimmy gazed back out the window. The rain quickly picked up intensity, and within seconds was falling in torrents. He could almost sense its rage, the fury with which it fell, the water like knives tearing through the skies. He could feel his muscles clenching, and he knew that he would have to sit this one out if he wanted to maintain his strength.

"I can handle it," Tara Frey said, eyes closed as her voice came in a soft whisper. "You've done enough for one night."

"So have you," Jimmy replied. "I don't believe this one will be easy to overcome."

Tara opened her eyes and smiled at her son, her face calm. "It has never been easy."

Jimmy didn't reply, only stared out into the rain.

"Have you chosen?" Tara asked, slowly getting up and reaching for her shoes.

Jimmy watched her intently, his admiration for her growing as he felt her fight through her exhaustion and ready herself. "Yes," he finally said, "although I'm not so sure."

Tara turned and smiled at her son. "You'll figure it out," she said.

Jimmy smiled back as his mother crossed to where he sat, bent down and kissed his forehead.

"I love you, Jimmy Frey," she said, running her hand across his cheek. "No matter what."

Jimmy nodded and watched as his mother opened the door to their room and stepped out into the storm.

***

Jason Collick was going mad.

The voices were clearer now, angrier, hissing in his ear and echoing in his mind. He fought to clear his head, to rid himself of their incessant accusations and attacks, but his efforts were useless. The blood in his temples was throbbing dangerously, making his eyes water as he staggered back and forth through the room, trying to fight off the hammering in his head.

Jason leaned against the wall, exhausted and in pain. He knocked his head against the hard surface, hoping that the shock would send the voices away. His hand reached out for the door knob, twisted it angrily, praying for an escape. The door was locked and Jason cried out in frustration.

"You won't escape again!"

A loud thud came from his right, and Jason's eyes grew wide when he stared into the dead eyes of a man in a business suit, standing just outside the window. He was smiling, his face pressed against the window, his mouth open in a silent cry of anger. His fingernails scratched at the window, wanting to get in, and Jason quickly staggered away from him.

A hand grabbed the collar of Jason's shirt and pulled him to the floor, a heavy body quickly straddling him. On any other day, Jason would have found the woman beautiful, if not for the black eyes and tears of blood streaming down her cheeks. She bent close, her hands holding him down by the shoulders, her strength inconsistent with her form. Jason could smell the rot on her breath as she locked her lips onto his, then bit hard enough to draw blood.

"We missed you, Jason," she sneered. "Did you miss us? Do you remember us?"

Jason panicked and kicked out, pushing the woman off him and rolling away, putting distance between them. When he looked back, she was gone.

And still, the voices came.

Jason cried out, drawing his knees to his chest and burying his face in his hands. The pain was incredible, pouring through him as if a hundred knives were cutting across his skin. He didn't know how much of this he could take.

The walls around him suddenly began to pulsate, matching his heartbeats as they bulged and retracted. Hands broke through them, followed by decaying arms and flapping skin. One by one, Jason watched as the room filled with the dead, tens of them, climbing out of the wall and smiling wickedly as they advanced on him.

Jason quickly crawled to his suitcase, frantically digging his hand inside and searching.

"Confess!"

Jason found his gun, pulled it out and aimed it at the empty room with shaky hands. The dead were gone, but the voices in his head were not.

"Do it!"

Jason forced his eyes shut, slamming the butt of his gun against his temple in an attempt to rid himself of the hissing whispers.

"Pull the trigger, Jason! End it now!"

Jason screamed and raised his gun, firing two shots into the ceiling, bits of plaster raining down on his head.

The voices disappeared.

Jason opened his eyes, feeling the strain in his head disappear. His vision cleared, but his breathing was still coming in gasps and his heart pounded hard in his chest. He stood up slowly, the gun at his head rattling as his hand shook uncontrollably. He took a few tentative steps forward, eyes searching for any signs of more attacks to come.

When he was sure he was alone, he relaxed. He took in deep breaths, letting them out in long, strenuous exhales as he massaged the tightness in his chest. He could still smell rot in the air, and his shoulders were throbbing with pain where the woman had grabbed him and pinned him down. Yet all that didn't matter; all that was bearable. At least they were gone.

"Confess, Jason."

The voice came from behind him, and Jason quickly turned, his gun raised threateningly. A figure was standing in the bathroom, half hidden in the dark. It chuckled lightly.

"Guns won't work here."

The figure moved into the light, slowly. The man stood tall, almost as tall as Jason, clad in a suit drenched in water, the right side of his face hanging down in flaps of skin. One bloody eye stared at Jason angrily, the empty socket beside it just as terrorizing. The man was smiling, a toothless smile as water trickled out of his mouth.

"Confess, my friend."

Jason recognized his old partner immediately. "Chuck?" he stammered.

Chuck threw his head back and laughed hysterically, the water in his mouth gurgling and forcing him to cough. He ran a hand through the few strands of hair left on his head as he took a few more steps towards Jason.

"Confess!" Chuck hissed. "Look at me. Look at what you did to me, and confess!"

Jason shook his head, closing his eyes and opening them again, hoping that this was just another vision. Chuck didn't disappear, the man's smile only widening.

"Go!" Jason yelled at him. "I'll shoot, I swear!"

Chuck laughed again. "I believe you," he said, his tone suddenly serious. "You've done it before."

Jason took a few steps back, his hand finding the door and turning the knob. To his relief, it opened.

"Confess!" Chuck screeched and immediately lunged at Jason.

Jason pulled the trigger twice.

*** 

Owen Little made his way towards the maintenance room.

The rain was coming down hard, and he was barely halfway to his destination before he could feel the water soak into his socks and underwear.

*Damn this night!*

He had been awakened earlier by the screaming actress, pulled out of another deep slumber and cursing the gods for his misfortune. He had raced out of his room just as the actress was being escorted out of her room, everyone crowded around her and comforting her, as if she needed more attention. It disgusted Owen, and when he saw the broken door, his repulsion had spiked even more.

Now he was forced to repair the damn thing before the rain ruined the furniture inside. Normally, he would have called Sal to do the job, but there was still no coverage, and he didn't want to be face to face with the man when he told him what to do. Owen knew Sal wouldn't be happy about it, especially since he already had a deep distaste for the young actress after their run-in at the pool.

Owen looked up at the renovated rooms as he walked past them. He had hoped they'd be done by now, but business was slow. The entire wing looked forlorn and uninviting, especially during a night like this, and he toyed with the idea of cutting down costs by finishing some of the repairs himself. He could probably drag Sal along with him. The man would give him hell, but Sal was a loyal dog, and Owen had no doubt he'd probably do a better job than anyone else.

The door to the maintenance room stood open and a dim light burned inside. Owen made his way in, walking around the large shelves and smiling to himself when he saw Sal bent over the workstation.

"I was looking for you," Owen lied.

Sal looked over his shoulder and scoffed. "You coulda tried my phone."

"No coverage," Owen said as he walked up to the man and looked down at what he was working on.

Sal had his watch open, the wheels, barrel and ratchet all lined up neatly to one side as he worked. "The clocks ain't working, either," Sal said. "Digital or any o'the others. Damn storm's sent us back to the stone ages."

"The televisions still work, and we have electricity," Owen pointed out.

"Yippidy friggin' doo-da!" Sal spat.

Owen walked over to one of the shelves and sifted through the boxes there, looking for a new doorknob.

"That actress you ran into earlier," Owen said. "Diana something-something."

Sal scoffed. "Little daddy's girl."

"Yeah, well, her door just lost a knob," Owen said. "Another guest kicked it in when they heard screaming."

Sal dropped his tools and stood up straight, looking at Owen angrily. "An' I'm supposed to stand in that damn weather and fix it?"

"That is your job, Sal," Owen said, finding what he wanted and tossing it to the man.

Sal let the knob hit him and drop to the floor. "I ain't doin' shit for that bitch."

"It's not a request," Owen said, gesturing to the knob on the floor. "Get it done when you're finished here."

Owen made to leave when Sal stopped him. "I'm gonna need the keys to the truck."

"Why?" Owen asked, a little agitated that he was spending more time here than he needed to.

"Need to drive into town," Sal said. "We need batteries and parts to fix the clocks. An' we lost two generators. We ain't gonna have electricity in the morning if we lose the third."

Owen cursed. It was just his luck. More costs just kept piling up on him. He made a mental note to charge Diana for the broken door.

"I'll drive into town," Owen said. "You see to that door, and let Connor know he's in charge until I get back."

Sal sniffed and spat as Owen walked back out into the rain.

***

Gina Andrews felt like she was in high school again.

It wasn't the pretty actress sitting next to her and being ogled at by everyone in the bar, with herself completely invisible. Gina was used to getting little to no attention from men, other than those who wanted her money, and she had gotten used to the rejection over the years. She couldn't say that it didn't bother her, but she wasn't prone to locking herself up in her room and crying about it anymore.

No, it had more to do with how she felt around Diana. Suddenly, she was transported back to her school cafeteria, sitting alone with her food, looking longingly at the cliques of girls sitting around her. She remembered the feeling of wanting to walk up and ask to be their friend. She remembered her need for acceptance, and that if somehow she could get their approval, she would immediately be regarded as *cool*.

She felt the same way now, sitting next to Diana, trying to comfort her while at the same time hoping that her efforts would be appreciated and the two of them would somehow hit it off. She scolded herself, wondering how, after all these years, after all this success, she still needed recognition.

Besides, it wasn't like she was ever going to meet any of these people again. As far as she was concerned, she would be long gone the minute the sun came up. She didn't need any of the other guests' approval, let alone Diana's. Yet Gina couldn't help herself, and she whispered and cooed as much as she could to make the woman feel as comfortable as possible.

"Can you stop touching me?" Diana suddenly said, her first words since they had helped her out of her room.

Gina felt the words like a slap to the face. "I'm sorry," she muttered, immediately regretting her apology and wincing at how pathetic she sounded. Her mother would have had a ball if she were here. "I was just trying to help."

"Yeah, well, you're kind of suffocating me," Diana said, shifting her chair a few inches away from Gina. She was obviously feeling much better, the initial shock of what had happened gone and replaced with a sense of self-importance.

Gina's cheeks flushed in embarrassment. "Are you sure you're okay?" she asked nevertheless, hating herself for it.

Diana gave her a disgusted look. "Don't you have a sandwich to eat or something?"

Gina stood up angrily, tears stinging her eyes, and raced out of the bar.

\*\*\*

"I'm tellin' you, you don't want him in charge during this storm."

Owen shook his head in frustration. He fought the urge to turn around and blow up in Sal's face. Not tonight. Especially not tonight, when he couldn't afford to anger Sal. He needed the man's full support to keep the entire motel from breaking down. The storm didn't seem like it was going to let up, and Owen had to admit that without Sal, he'd be lost.

"He ain't got any idea about anythin'," Sal was saying.

"It's for an hour, Sal," Owen yelled over his shoulder. "Take it easy."

"He's gonna get ideas, that one," Sal said. "Leavin' him in charge all the time is gonna get to his head, and soon he'll want the motel to himself."

Owen stopped and turned to face the man. "Ease up, alright?" he hissed. "I gave you a job to do, so instead of harassing me with this nonsense, get it done."

"I knew a man once," Sal said. "Things got to his head, too, that one. Did some terrible things to get what he wanted." Sal leaned in close. "Dragged others along with 'im."

Owen felt the anger boil up inside him. He closed the gap between him and Sal, looking up into the man's eyes. "Get to work," he said through clenched teeth, then turned and walked towards the truck.

Owen knew what Sal was thinking, always jealous of how much more Owen trusted Connor over him. He couldn't deny Sal's worth to the motel and knew he would do everything he could to keep the man happy, but sometimes Sal pushed it. Besides, how could he trust him? After everything that had happened, he would be a fool to give his back to the man.

Owen climbed into the truck and slammed the door behind him. Pulling out his keys, he squinted through the rain at Sal standing several feet away, completely still, watching him. Owen would never hear the end of this, but for now, they all had work to do, and apparently the storm would not let them rest until the morning.

His eye caught movement, and he frowned at the figure of a woman running across the second floor landing. Owen knew it couldn't be the actress, or the other woman with the red hair. It could only be the woman from earlier, the mother who had been waiting for a cab with her son. What the hell was she doing out in this weather?

Owen shook his head. If anything else happened, it wasn't his responsibility anymore. Connor would handle it.

He turned the ignition, shifted into drive and pulled out of his parking space. He barely looked at Sal as he turned to the left and maneuvered his vehicle towards the exit. The rain fell hard against the windshield, and Owen switched on the wipers, wincing at the sound of rubber against glass. The neon sign of the Kurtain Motel flickered as he drove past it.

"Darling, really, you should wear your seatbelt."

Owen's eyes shot up to the rearview mirror and the reflection of his dead wife smiling back at him. Her hair had fallen out completely, and her skin had turned grey with decay. She gave him a wide smile, and from behind her lips, a torrent of black beetles crawled out.

"Confess!" she giggled, reaching for him.

Owen swerved.

*****

Sal watched the truck head towards the exit, almost disappearing in the sheets of rain falling around him.

He hated Owen. After all he had done for that man, after getting his hands dirty, he was still being treated like trash. Without him, Owen would have still been his wife's slave. Mrs. Little had been gentler, albeit naïve and a little too generous. She had been driving the motel into the ground, and when Owen approached him with a plan, Sal had instantly jumped at the opportunity to prove he was more than just the 'super'.

Now, though, he felt more and more like he had been used. Nothing had changed since he helped Owen get rid of the missus. On the contrary, things had only gotten worse for him. And now, Connor was slowly becoming Owen's right hand man instead of him.

Sal's mind raced with ideas of what he wanted to do to Owen, of how he would get what he deserved.

Sudden gunshots startled him, and Sal turned in alarm as one of the guests raced out of his room and into the rain. The man was hysterical, the gun in his hand raised and aimed at the room as if waiting for someone to follow him out.

"You're dead!" the man screamed, letting off another two shots. The sound was deafening as it echoed across the motel.

"Hey!" Sal shouted, flinching at the sound of the gunshot, waving his arms to get the man's attention. "Hey, are you insane?"

The man looked at him, startled, then quickly raised his gun.

Sal was about to duck when a sudden blinding light came from his left.

\*\*\*

Jason Collick shook in fear as the rain fell around him, his arm raised as he aimed his gun at the advancing figure of Chuck.

"Confess!" Chuck yelled through the storm.

"You're dead!" Jason screamed, pulling the trigger twice as he staggered backwards.

"Hey!"

Jason turned instinctively, and his heart almost stopped.

"Hey, are you insane!"

A man was waving his arms at him, and all around him, hundreds of dead stood stoically in the rain. Men, women and children, like marble statues poised in his direction, each and every one staring at him in fury. One of them stepped forward, and Jason quickly shifted his aim, ready to shoot.

Then they were gone, and Jason was left standing alone, staring in horror as a truck slammed into the waving man.

\*\*\*

Owen Little had no idea what happened.

One second he was driving out of the motel, and the next, his entire world was turned upside down. The hissing sounds of his wife coming for him from the truck's backseat lingered in his head, and the image of the beetles crawling out of her mouth was still fresh in his mind. He remembered swerving, aiming for the field just outside the motel.

But, for some strange reason, he was driving back into the Kurtain Motel. Sal had appeared out of nowhere, and Owen was too slow to react. There was a loud thump as he slammed into the man and sent him flying forward, the sound of breaking bones loud in the falling rain.

Owen screeched to a stop and jumped out of the truck, racing toward Sal frantically. Someone was screaming, a woman, and Owen barely took notice of the man staring at him in shock with a gun in his hand, shaking uncontrollably.

Owen fell to his knees next to Sal's limp body, the man's eyes wide as he stared out into space, his breath coming in gasps. His left leg was bent at an impossible angle, and Owen could see the bone sticking out from the man's thigh.

"You hit me!" Sal stammered.

Owen shook his head, trying to clear his mind. He looked up at the man with the gun, still shaking and probably completely useless right now. Owen looked past him and waved frantically at Gina.

"Get help!" Owen yelled at her.

Gina hesitated, and Owen cursed out at her. "Now!"

Gina turned and ran towards the bar.

Owen looked down at Sal, holding the man's hand tight as they gazed into each other's eyes.

"You son of a bitch!" Sal coughed. "You tried to kill me!"

"Sal, I–"

"I'm gonna see you in cuffs for this!" Sal hissed.

Owen stared at the man in shock, unable to make any sense of what had just happened. He glanced up at the truck, headlights shining bright in his eyes.

His wife was sitting in the passenger seat, smiling at him.

## Chapter 10

"I'm telling you, I wasn't even supposed to be in the motel!"

Patrick Lahm tried to make sense of what Owen was saying. The man was sweating profusely, rubbing his hands together as he sat fidgeting in his seat. All eyes were on him, and Patrick could see that he didn't like being the center of attention; right now, he would probably have been more comfortable under a rock.

Gina's screams echoed in Patrick's head. They had practically slammed into her on their way out of the bar, and it had taken Harold a good while to try and calm her down while the rest of them ran to see what had happened. Patrick knew it would be a long time before he could forget the image of Sal on the ground, bleeding with his thigh bone sticking out like a flag post.

"I was driving *out* of the motel," Owen was saying. "I have no idea what happened!"

Patrick glanced at Harold, an eyebrow raised, hoping that the priest could make better sense of what they were hearing.

"Connor!" Owen cried out. "Connor, you believe me, don't you? You have to believe me!"

Connor shrugged, equally uneasy as the rest of the guests in the bar gazed at him. It had taken the combined strength of both him and Patrick to get Owen off of Sal, and even then Owen was kicking out and screaming that it was an accident, that he had not seen Sal in the rain.

"Sorry, boss, but you aren't making a lot of sense," Connor muttered.

Owen gazed at him angrily, ready to jump the man if not for Cameron standing between the two of them.

Cameron clicked his tongue and moved closer to Patrick, leaning in as he whispered, "I told you, man, this place is messed up."

Patrick ignored the comment. Right now, he was more worried about Sal than anything else. The telephones weren't working, and nobody at the Kurtain Motel had cell phone coverage. They had carried Sal into his room where Gina had offered to stay and watch him until they could find a way to get him to a hospital. No one was willing to take the risk of moving the man any more than needed; there was no telling what other injuries he had sustained from the collision. All they could do was try and stop the bleeding until a solution could be found.

"How far is the next town?" Patrick asked Owen, snapping his fingers to get the man's attention.

Owen frowned in concentration. "Ten miles, a little more."

Patrick looked up at the others and shrugged. "Anyone willing to drive?"

"We can take my car," Harold said. "I suggest you join me, though. Two pairs of eyes guiding us through this storm are better than one."

Patrick nodded and looked back at Owen. The man was staring out into space. No doubt what he had done was just starting to sink in, the realization that he was probably the reason for another man's death. An employee, for that matter. Patrick could only imagine what was going on inside his head.

"What do we do about him?" Cameron asked, gesturing towards Jason Collick sitting at another table, arms wrapped around his shoulders as he rocked back and forth.

Patrick almost forgot about him. He remembered Kurt telling them that the man had a stick up his ass the size of an obelisk, and the fact that he had been standing in the rain with a gun in his hand made everyone uneasy. Even though Kurt had unarmed him without any incident, they had all agreed that the gun was to stay with Connor at all times.

Patrick frowned at Jason, watching him intently. Although he was rocking in his seat, his eyes were staring at them lifelessly. Gina's cries for help must have brought him out, but Patrick had a hard time believing that someone willing to wield a gun would be affected this much by the accident.

Unless there was something else.

Things were starting to escalate at the Kurtain Motel, and more and more of it made very little sense. Patrick began to wonder if maybe there were some truth to Cameron's theory; maybe the motel really was haunted. He didn't want to put too much thought into it yet, but there was no denying that he would have to keep the possibility in mind. So much couldn't be explained otherwise.

"We'll wait here," Connor said, eyeing Jason. "I'll keep an eye on that one."

Patrick nodded and led Harold out of the bar. The rain was still coming down hard, and after recent events, it was giving the motel a much more ominous mood than before. He hadn't minded the weather as much when they had first arrived, but it was really starting to get to him now.

They sprinted across the parking lot with Patrick only giving the truck a brief glance before shuddering and pressing on. He didn't want to think of the accident now, or of Owen's strange explanation. All he wanted to do was find help, and quick.

*Besides, an hour or two away from this place would be good,* he thought to himself.

"I hope you're sober enough," Harold joked as he unlocked the car doors.

Patrick gave him a thumbs-up as he jumped into the passenger seat beside him. Harold closed his door, stuck the key in the ignition and turned. The car sputtered and coughed, but wouldn't start. Harold frowned and tried again, pumping the gas. Still, nothing happened.

"Battery dead?" Patrick asked, silently cursing their luck.

Harold shook his head in confusion. "I don't know. Seems like it." He tried again, the lights on the dashboard flickering with the effort, then dying. "This makes no sense."

"I guess we're both going to need help in the morning," Patrick said, forcing a weak smile.

Harold looked out at the other parked cars. "Do you think we can borrow someone else's car?"

"I'm not sure," Patrick replied. "Won't hurt to ask."

Harold nodded. "I'll be right back," he said, stepping out and racing towards the bar.

Patrick blew into his cupped hands and rubbed them together. The temperature had dropped significantly, although it was still early fall, and the combination of cold and rain was not doing his body any good. If he did make it to the book signing in time, he was probably going to spend it blowing his nose and sneezing into the crook of his elbow.

A light tapping startled him. It came from inside the car, quite distinct from the rain tapping against the vehicle's frame. It was soon joined by a second set of tapping, and then a third, and in seconds, dozens more. Patrick looked about anxiously, wondering what was causing the sound, when he felt something crawling up his left arm.

Patrick jumped at the sight of the spider, its legs sending goose bumps up and down the length of his arm as he quickly brushed it off him. It disappeared under the driver's seat, scurrying away as the tapping sounds intensified. Patrick's eyes grew wide when another spider crawled out of the air conditioning vents, quickly followed by more.

"Confess!"

The voice was in his ear, the whisper a strong hiss that pierced through his head. Patrick knew he couldn't be dreaming this. He fumbled with the door handle, trying to get out of the car as the spiders kept coming. Some found their way up his pants and he frantically swatted at them. The door flew open and Patrick fell in a heap onto the wet ground, pushing himself away from the car. He watched in horror as the spiders crawled out after him, and without thinking twice, he kicked the door shut.

"What are you doing?"

Patrick turned to look at the woman watching him from under the shelter of the canopy. Her hair was tied back, and her eyes were a light grey that appeared to shimmer in the dim light around her. He remembered the last time he had seen her, at the front desk with her son, that same look on her face.

Patrick looked back at Harold's car, but the spiders were gone. "Nothing," he said, glancing at the woman and smiling. "I thought I saw something."

The woman's eyes moved between the car and Patrick.

"You're Jimmy's mother, right?" Patrick asked, pushing himself to his feet and hurrying out of the rain.

"Tara," she replied, nodding as she watched him closely.

Kurt was right; she really was a striking woman. Patrick noted the high cheekbones and the curved lips, a strand of brown hair escaping her ponytail and falling lazily across the side of her face. He could see where Jimmy got his looks and wondered if the boy was out in the rain as well.

"Quite a kid you have," Patrick said. "Ran into him a couple of times."

Tara didn't reply. She stared out at Harold's car, then back at Patrick. "You should go back inside," she said. "The night isn't very friendly."

"Yeah, my thoughts exactly," Patrick said, "but we have to get help. I don't know if you heard, but there was an accident earlier."

"I saw it," Tara said. "The man's beyond help."

Patrick was surprised by how cold her tone was. "He's not exactly in the best possible state," he said. "Doesn't mean we should just sit around and wait for him to die."

Tara shook her head. "You misunderstand me," she said. "I meant you won't be able to find help for him."

Patrick hadn't wanted to consider it before, but now that Tara said it out loud, he had to admit that it was a possibility. There was no telling what they would find once they reached the next town.

"The weather's definitely a hurdle," he said, more to himself than to her.

"So is the motel," Tara added.

Patrick looked at her in confusion. "Excuse me?"

Tara gave him a small smile, and Patrick felt a shudder rush through him. "I can see why he chose you," she said. "Good luck, Patrick Lahm. You'll need it."

"Patrick!"

Patrick turned to the sound of Harold calling, the priest rushing towards him through the rain with his coat pulled up over his head, followed closely by Kurt.

"Confess!"

Patrick turned back to Tara, but the woman was gone.

\*\*\*

"This is how we're doing it, period!"

Jason Collick slammed his hand down hard, and the conference room fell into a vacuum-like silence. Eyes stared at him in shock. He gazed out at the men and women sitting around him, his brows furrowed, his teeth clenched. He shot daggers at them, challenging anyone to speak up, and only relaxed when he realized his anger had the desired effect.

Jason was known for having a level head, for being incredibly cold in the face of all matters concerning the million-dollar company. It was a character trait that annoyed many. He was a difficult man to anger, everyone knew that, which made his sudden outburst even more surprising.

But Jason knew this would be the first of many. He was losing his temper quicker these days, sleeping less, obsessing about the little stuff and, in general, spiraling completely out of control. He started seeing a therapist, the early signs of uncontrolled anger forcing him to seek out professional help, but he was just two sessions in and only getting worse.

He was feeling a lot more paranoid as well, as if someone were always out to get him. Recently, he had caught himself looking over his shoulder during his morning jogs and double-checking the locks on his door before going to sleep. Last week, he had even bought a gun.

"I've made up my mind, and I don't want any more discussions on the issue," Jason said, lowering his voice as he settled back down into his chair.

"Sir, we're talking fraud here," his CFO said, visibly uncomfortable. "If we don't find a solution, a lot of people will lose their money."

Jason didn't reply. He knew what was at stake. It was moments like these he wished Chuck were still alive to handle things. Jason wasn't a man of the people, and he wasn't delusional either. When push came to shove, he would probably falter. His last hope was next month's meeting. They needed new investors.

"How do we look with SratTech?" Jason asked.

The men and women at the table looked at each other anxiously, no one willing to speak their mind about the failing venture. It was a take-over that had cost the company millions and was bringing in close to nothing. Chuck had been right; it was a stupid idea, even though Jason still had hopes that he could prove everyone wrong.

"Somebody say something," Jason said through clenched teeth, fighting back the rage threatening to explode again.

"The numbers don't look good," the CFO replied, taking on the mantle of spokesperson for what everyone else was too scared to say. "If we don't sell it off soon, we're only going to see more loss in the next quarter."

"The new software that they're working on should bring the numbers up," Jason said.

"If they had stuck to deadlines," the CFO replied. "Plans leaked, and the competition's already got a prototype out. At the current pace, we'll be playing catch-up forever."

Jason sighed. He could see it on their faces, all of them looking to him for a solution deep down they knew he didn't have. None of them had faith that he could pull them out of eventual bankruptcy, and their thoughts on the matter might as well have been written across their foreheads. Still, they held their tongues.

"Light a fire under them," Jason said. "Double shifts if they have to."

"We can't afford to pay people for overtime," the CFO replied. "We're already losing a lot of money as is."

"Just do it!" Jason shouted.

Everyone seemed to flinch at the same time, and Jason could easily see the sudden look of fear on their faces.

*That's it,* he thought. *I've lost them completely.*

Jason stood up, adjusted his suit jacket and collected the files in front of him, storming out of the conference room without another word.

## Chapter 11

Kurt Layton turned the key in the ignition and pressed down several times on the gas. For a second, it seemed like his car would start, the engine giving a quick kick before dying. He looked out at Harold and Patrick and shrugged.

"What are the odds?" Harold clicked his tongue.

Patrick glanced towards Tara Frey's room, the light soft behind the drawn curtains. A part of him wanted to believe that she had nothing to do with their current predicament, but the coincidence was a little too much to ignore. Diana's car had a flat and no spare, and Gina's gas light had flashed on the minute they had tried to take hers.

"Connor?" Patrick asked.

"No one's going to drive the truck after what happened," Harold shook his head.

"And I assume gun-toting Joe is out of the question?"

"You assume correctly."

Patrick sighed and scratched the back of his head. "How many miles did Owen say it was to the next town?"

"Ten," Harold replied. He turned to look at Patrick. "I highly advise not doing what you're thinking of doing."

"We don't have any other option."

"Yes, we do," Harold said. "We wait until the morning. Walking in this weather is a fool's journey."

"Sal could be dead by the morning," Patrick argued.

"And you think you can walk ten miles and get back before that?" Harold asked, a deep scowl on his face. "Don't be ridiculous. You'd only be putting yourself in harm's way."

"It's worth a shot," Patrick said, already making up his mind.

He didn't want to tell Harold how he really felt, that he didn't believe it would be morning any time soon. After what Tara had said to him, he was starting to feel more and more like they were in some kind of twilight zone. He knew that walking to town was stupid, but right now he just wanted to prove to himself that he could leave, that the motel wasn't actually trying to keep them in.

Kurt got out of his car and quickly joined them under the canopy. "Sorry, fellas, I really thought I could get it to work that time," he said.

"Don't worry about it," Patrick said. "You wouldn't happen to have a flashlight in there, would you?"

Kurt eyed him. "Matter of fact, I do," he said. "You ain't thinking of walking, are you?"

Harold scoffed before Patrick could reply.

Kurt shook his head and smiled. "You're out of your mind."

"Only solution we've got," Patrick said. "I can't sit around here and do nothing."

Kurt licked his lips and nodded. He rushed back to his car, opened the trunk and rummaged around a bit before returning with the flashlight. He handed it to Patrick.

"You're actually condoning this?" Harold asked.

Kurt shrugged. "A man's gotta do what a man's gotta do," he said. "He's already made up his mind, Father." He looked at Patrick and winked. "If the storm gets any worse, you find shelter and settle down until we come get you, you hear?"

"Sure," Patrick said.

"Good luck," Harold said. "You'll need it."

Patrick hesitated, remembering that Tara had said the same thing to him just moments before. He raised the torch in a mock salute, smiled at the two men, and walked away.

\*\*\*

They were everywhere.

Jason Collick rocked in his seat, his eyes darting back and forth as he fought the inner urge to scream. The dead sat at the tables, stood in various corners, some even propped up on the bar stools. They were all staring at him, their eyes dark and menacing, their scowls enough to drive him mad.

He needed to get out. Before Chuck arrived.

"Hey, man, you alright? You're looking kind of pale."

Jason froze, his eyes flying open as Chuck's face materialized from in between the rest of the dead. He instantly felt his entire body go numb, and his eyes darted for the door. The dead around him smiled.

"Confess now, Jason. Confess and all will be forgiven."

Jason stared at his dead partner as the man approached, water dripping off his suit onto the bar floor, his eyes hollow sockets. It was like looking into the pits of hell. Jason wanted to scream, but he knew that was what they wanted. They wanted him to squirm. They wanted him to beg for forgiveness. But, he wouldn't do that. He wouldn't give them the satisfaction.

"Dude, you okay?"

Jason needed his gun. He looked over at the bartender who had taken it from him, the big man watching intently as Chuck approached Jason, unmoving. They were in on it. Everyone was in on it. The rest of the guests knew his secret and were tormenting him along with the ghosts around him. Jason felt his anger well up, promising himself that he would not falter. He would not give into these games. He was going to come out on top. He always did.

"Confess!" Chuck hissed, water bursting out from his mouth. Jason's eyes fell to his partner's chest where two red spots had suddenly appeared, spreading out until they fused together and covered the entire front of his shirt.

"Confess!"

"Leave me alone!" Jason screamed.

\*\*\*

Cameron staggered, jolted by the man's sudden outburst. He looked at Connor who waved at him to step away. Cameron looked back at Jason, frowning.

"I was just worried about you, man," he said. "No need to get angry."

"Get away from me," Jason hissed, baring his teeth. "You're dead, you hear me? You're dead!"

Cameron threw his hands up in frustration and walked back to the bar. He pulled himself up on the stool, briefly looking over his shoulder at Jason before shaking his head in disbelief.

"Can you believe this guy?" he asked Connor.

Connor shrugged and continued cleaning the glass in his hand. "Still in shock, I guess."

"Good thing he doesn't have the gun," Cameron said. "Who knows what he'd do with that thing."

"He looks harmless," Connor said. "Besides, if he was going to use it, he would have already."

"Yeah, well I feel a lot more comfortable now that it's with you."

Connor said nothing and just stared at Jason from across the bar.

\*\*\*

Patrick couldn't see through the rain. He knew it was impossible, and for a few seconds, he had actually believed the storm picked up the closer he got to the motel exit. A cold wind blew against him, forcing the rain painfully against his face, and he was forced to close his eyes as he made his way forward.

The lights were still on in the office, and it acted as his lighthouse in this storm. He felt like he had been walking forever, although he knew that if he were to look back, he would find that he was no more than twenty yards away from where he had started. Yet, the feeling was there.

The neon sign of the Kurtain Motel loomed in front of him, lights flickering on and off as the sign swayed in the wind. He quickly ducked under the front office canopy, hoping for some shelter from the weather's onslaught during the last few yards, but the storm followed. The wind rushed at him from every direction, the rain hitting him like rubber bullets against his cheeks and neck.

*This is absurd.*

Patrick pulled the collar of his coat up higher and pressed on, determined now more than ever to leave. If the motel really was keeping them here, he needed to see it for himself. He hardly believed Owen's story, and he didn't care how cryptic Tara and her son were being. The truth of the matter was that a man was dying and needed help.

Patrick wasn't going to let bad weather slow him down. He braced himself and dashed out of the canopy's cover. He raced passed the flickering neon sign, his eyes looking past the curtain of rain and at the highway beyond, when everything suddenly went dark.

Patrick couldn't explain it, but for a split second, it was as if he were suspended in a dark void, his legs touching nothing beneath him, his movements slow and heavy. He gasped for air, the darkness around him a deep vacuum that threatened to suffocate him. He felt his chest burn, his mind completely numb, and that was when the hand grabbed him.

He couldn't see it, but he definitely felt it. Fingers wrapped around the front collar of his shirt, grasping tight, and pulled him forward. There was a loud popping sound in his ears, and he was suddenly propelled forward, landing hard on his hands and knees.

The rain had stopped, but the wind still hit at him, the cold reaching into his coat and seeping down his back. Patrick gasped for breath, feeling like he had spent an eternity in the void, the murkiness of it still heavy on his skin. He coughed and spat, his chest still burning as he slowly pushed himself up to his feet.

"Patrick?"

Patrick looked up, and even though he was surrounded by darkness, the moonlight was enough for him to make out the shocked look on Harold Bell and Kurt Layton's faces.

***

Connor was wiping down the bar when the lights went out.

Cameron had been dragging on and on about his baseball career, but Connor was barely listening. He was more amused by how quickly the kid had given up all attempts at keeping his identity a secret, chatting away excitedly as if he had been locked away and finally found people to talk to. Connor wasn't interested, though, his concentration more on the man in the corner and Owen.

"What the hell?" Cameron called out, annoyed that he had been so abruptly interrupted.

Connor sighed. He had a feeling this would happen, especially since nothing had been done to fix the roof of the generator room since the last storm had brought their attention to the leaks. Connor knew it was only a matter of time before the rain would get in, but had hoped that they could at least make it through the night without having to worry about feeling their way around in the dark.

"I thought you said this place had back-up generators," Cameron said.

"We were working on those," Owen replied as Connor turned instinctively towards the drawer behind him and took out the candles stocked up inside. "We lost power hours ago when the storm first hit."

"And now the generators are a bust?"

Connor took out his lighter and lit the first candle, setting it near the small sink. "Sal's responsible for making sure this doesn't happen," he said, lighting a second. "I guess we're on our own now."

Cameron shook his head in disbelief and leaned over the bar, grabbing one of the glasses and a bottle of whiskey. He poured himself a drink and downed it before refilling his glass.

"Just when I needed the bathroom, too," he said, reaching out a hand and beckoning Connor for a candle.

Connor handed one to him and pointed to the left. "Just watch your step, alright? We don't need any more accidents."

Cameron scoffed and slid off his seat, holding the candle in front of him as he walked away. Connor watched him disappear before turning back to light another stick.

"I hope he trips and breaks his neck in there," Owen muttered in the darkness. "I'm going to shoot myself if I have to listen to another one of his stories."

Connor made his way around the bar and set a candle in front of his boss, looking at him disapprovingly.

"Not really the best time to be saying things like that," Connor remarked.

"Sal was an accident," Owen said, his head lowered and his eyes sunken in the dim glow of the candlelight.

"I know that," Connor replied, "but the rest of these folks don't. If I were you, boss, I'd keep my thoughts to myself right now."

Owen looked up angrily, about to reply, when his eyes suddenly grew wide. Connor registered the expression a second too late, the blow against his head blacking him out immediately as he fell forward and collapsed onto the table.

*** 

Jimmy Frey stood silently in the dark, leaning against the railing as he watched the three men below. He had witnessed Patrick's attempt to leave the motel, how one second the man was walking out, and in the next, falling back in. He could sense the confusion, disbelief, and the utter frustration, but he kept his mouth shut. There was no need to draw attention to himself right now. It would only complicate what had to be done.

Tara walked up behind him and placed a hand on his shoulder.

"You pulled him out," Jimmy said, glancing back.

Tara nodded. "It wasn't easy," she said. "You were right about him."

Jimmy looked back at Patrick and smiled before pushing away from the railing and hugging his mother. The motel seemed a lot more eerie now that the power was out, but he felt safe in Tara's arms.

"You're putting too much pressure on yourself," he said. "You need to rest."

Tara smiled at her son and kissed his head. "When we're done here," she said. "I'll rest when it's all over."

Jimmy hugged her tighter and followed her into the room, closing the door behind them. He felt tingles run up and down his spine, excited about Patrick Lahm and what was to come. He had never met anyone like him before, and that just made it all the more interesting. He was curious to see what the man would do next.

"Don't turn on the lights," Tara said as Jimmy reached for the lamp by his side. "The power's out, remember?"

Jimmy nodded. Sometimes he forgot that he had to play along.

Tara smiled and turned to the bathroom when a sudden gasp escaped from her.

"What is it?" Jimmy asked, but he already knew the answer to his question. He felt it race through him as an image flashed before his eyes.

Jason Collick had his gun.

## Chapter 12

"So what's your deal?"

Gina glanced up at the actress. Diana was sitting on a chair by the window, having had moved it as close to the door as possible. The curtains were drawn, and the only light in the room came from the bedside lamp. Diana hadn't said a word since they brought Sal into the room, and she was useless when it came to taking care of him. Gina was left to carry the burden on her own, not that she minded much. It took her mind off of what she had seen.

"What do you mean?" Gina asked.

"I'm pretty good at reading people," Diana replied. "Every single one of the guests here seems to be hiding something, but you, you're different."

Gina took the towel off Sal's head, soaked it in the bucket by the bed, and replaced it. He had spiked a fever, which wasn't surprising, but definitely made things a lot more complicated. She was hoping help would arrive in time, because the way things looked now, Sal wasn't going to survive the night.

"I'm just a regular city girl," Gina said, giving Diana a weak smile.

"Bullshit," Diana replied. "You've got a baker's daughter look, and you're definitely a few pounds away from a heart attack, but you aren't regular."

Gina felt the woman's words cut at her, and she bit her lower lip in an attempt to stop herself from tearing up. It surprised her how much some things still hurt her.

"Take your car, for instance," Diana continued. "I'm not a fan of Bentleys, but it's an impressive car. And your shoes? Louis Vuitton, right?"

Gina glanced at her shoes and said nothing, instinctively hiding her heels under her chair. She had meant to change into sneakers earlier, but had apparently forgotten in the midst of all that was going on.

"Oh, come on, don't be coy," Diana said. "Flaunt your money for all I care. It definitely takes the edge off of everything else."

Gina felt she had had enough. "What is everything else?" she snapped, frowning at Diana.

Diana held up her hands in mock surrender. "Whatever," she said. "The world's a funny place, I guess."

Gina shook her head in disbelief. She was used to this kind of talk, petty jealousy from those who didn't have as much money as she did, people who obviously thought that just because she was overweight, she had to be down on her luck in every other department of her life as well. It angered her sometimes, but usually she just felt sorry for them.

Diana didn't deserve her pity, though, and Gina didn't intend to let her off so easily.

"So you're saying it isn't fair, is that it?" Gina pressed, eyeing the actress scornfully.

Diana looked at her for a beat before leaning forward, willing to take on the challenge. "No, it isn't," she said. "You have no idea what I had to go through to get where I am. I didn't have a silver spoon in my mouth the minute I was born."

Gina's eyes went wide. "Do you think I inherited this?" she asked in disbelief. "That's fresh. You say you worked hard? I bet you didn't have to do more than bat your pretty little eyelashes to get what you wanted. You're on every single billboard, flashing that smile of yours, posing all sexy for the camera. Even with your god-awful movies, you're still an American sweetheart. I might not know what you had to go through to become the fantasy of every teenage boy in the country, but don't presume to know what I've been through."

Gina stood up and marched to Diana, a finger pointed in the woman's face. "I know women like you, ex-cheerleaders who thought the world would bow to them once they left high school, but ended up in some trailer park doing some drunk man's laundry. I've had to deal with your kind all my life, and the one thing I won't put up with is your bigotry!"

Diana looked up at her angrily. "Get your finger out of my face before I break it," she hissed.

Gina smiled, feeling a rush of satisfaction race through her, knowing that she had gotten under the actress's skin. It was refreshing to see the pretty ones squirm. It didn't happen often, it was usually her mother who did the talking, but on the rare occasions she did stand up for herself, she loved every second of it. She could see the pain behind Diana's eyes, and she knew she had probably hit close to home.

"You want to stay in this room, then keep your opinions to yourself," Gina said, stepping back. "You're absolutely useless anyway."

Diana stared at the woman as she walked back to Sal's bedside and sat down, checking the dying man's bandages and soaking the towel on his head again. Diana felt the anger inside her well up, her hands clenched into fists that shook with rage. She had never thought she could hate someone this much, and for reasons beyond her, couldn't understand how she didn't have the upper hand over the woman.

Feeling like she couldn't let this slide, Diana stood up angrily, ready to tell Gina off, when the lights suddenly went out.

***

"What are we going to do, man?"

Cameron paced back and forth in a frantic frenzy, the hotel suite feeling much smaller as he imagined the walls closing in on him. His manager was on one knee next to the dead girl's body, checking for a pulse.

"She's dead, isn't she?" Cameron stammered. "Oh, man, she's dead, right?"

"Would you shut the hell up?" his manager snapped. Cameron watched him grab a towel and wipe his hands, tossing the stained cloth aside. "This is a whole different level of crap, Cameron."

"Man, we were just having fun," Cameron said. "How was I supposed to know she was overdosing?"

"Oh, I don't know," his manager looked at him angrily. "The vomiting of blood should have been a pretty sure sign!"

"Hey, man, don't talk to me like that!"

Cameron's eyes widened, surprised by how fast his manager got to his feet and grabbed him by the collar of his shirt.

"I suggest you shut the hell up so I can find a way to get you out of another one of your many messes," the man spat. He pushed Cameron onto the couch and pointed at him angrily. "Don't move!"

The manager took out his cellphone, looked at Cameron in disgust and made his way into another room.

Cameron shook in his place, feeling a sudden drop in the room's temperature. He glanced at the dead brunette lying on the floor a few feet away, her eyes staring lifelessly at the ceiling, her mouth caked in dried blood. She was one of the pretty ones, and wild enough to excite him into upping his dose tonight. Obviously, that had been a mistake.

He felt his pulse racing and his body began to shiver uncontrollably when his manager walked back in.

"Jesus, don't go into shock on me now," he said, grabbing a blanket off the couch and throwing it to Cameron. "I called for help. Try not to die on me before we're done cleaning this mess up."

Cameron wrapped himself in the blanket and tried to control his shaking. His manager cursed and took out his cellphone.

"Stay with me, kid!"

Before he could answer, Cameron's eyes rolled back in his head and he slumped down onto the floor beside the dead girl.

*\*\**

Cameron was washing his hands when he smelled the smoke.

At first, he thought it was from the candle, the light coming from it only enough to throw dark shadows across the walls of the bathroom. It had been a hurdle trying to piss with it in his hand, but he had quickly found a way to keep it balanced between the wall and a bar of soap. He looked at it, the black smoke rising from the flame, and realized that the scent couldn't have been this strong.

*Something's burning.*

Cameron quickly turned off the water and wiped his hands on his jeans. He ran a hand through his hair, gazing at his reflection in the mirror as he tried to comb loose strains into place with his fingers. The smell was getting heavier, and Cameron coughed as invisible fingers of smoke reached into his open mouth and down his throat, stinging him.

*What the hell's going on out there?*

"Confess."

The voice was barely a whisper, but in the empty bathroom, it echoed off the walls and sent shivers down his spine. He froze in his place, staring into the mirror as a form materialized behind him, stepping out from the shadows. Cameron felt his heart beat quicken as he gazed into the reflection of the smiling brunette, blood caked to her lips, white as a sheet even in the warm glow of the candlelight.

"Confess, Cameron," she whispered, seductively, dangerously.

Cameron jerked when her cold hand touched the nape of his neck, and he watched in horror as the candle dropped into the sink and went out, engulfing the bathroom in complete darkness.

"Confess."

Her lips were by his ear, her breath rotten, her whispers like nails against a blackboard. Cameron pushed away from the sink, blindly rushing to where he thought the door was. A hand ripped at his shirt, nails digging deep into his flesh as he pulled away while crying out in pain. He could feel the sting down his back as he was suddenly propelled forward, crashing hard against the wall as the woman's weight pushed against him.

She giggled behind him, a hand reaching forward and grabbing him where he didn't want to be grabbed, squeezing until he screamed and writhed against her.

"Confess," her haunting voice slithered into his ear. "Confess what you did to me. How you threw me out like a dog!"

Cameron placed both hands against the wall and pushed, throwing his weight back as he fell over and onto the bathroom floor. The woman's hand was gone, but her giggles only intensified until he was deafened by manic screams of delight. Cameron rolled onto his hands and knees, kicking as he jumped forward, slamming against the door and flinging himself outside.

The smoke instantly filled his lungs, and Cameron recoiled against the heat of the fire that was spreading through the bar. He caught sight of Owen pulling an unconscious Connor towards the exit, waving frantically for Cameron's help.

Cameron looked back over his shoulder, the light from the fire barely illuminating the bathroom. The woman stood in the doorway, her smile wide, twirling her fingers at him as she bit her lower lip.

"You're mine, Cameron," she giggled. "Tonight, you're all mine."

Cameron ran.

\*\*\*

"This is all beyond me, Patrick."

Harold stared out past the Kurtain Motel's entrance at the highway beyond. Patrick had tried to explain what had happened as best he could, hoping that his recalling of the few seconds in the void would make more sense to the priest than it did to him. Harold just shook his head in bewilderment, frowning as they both tried to fathom how Patrick was still inside the motel parking lot.

"Kurt?" Patrick looked at the older man, hoping for some help.

Kurt shrugged. "I've never seen anything like it," he said. "Makes me wonder if that Owen fella wasn't mad after all."

"You think the same thing happened to him?" Harold asked.

"It would explain what he was saying about not seeing Sal," Kurt replied, pulling out a rolled up cigarette and lighting it. The tip burned a bright orange in the otherwise dark motel.

Harold glanced at Patrick and shrugged, unable to find a better explanation.

"First things first," Kurt said. "We gotta do something about the power."

Patrick nodded as he looked about the dark motel. He had no idea when the lights had gone out, but it must have happened while he was in limbo. He remembered the neon sign flickering next to him when he was trying to leave.

"So, this void," Harold turned to look at Patrick. "You say someone pulled you out?"

Patrick was about to reply when Kurt tapped his shoulder urgently. "Fellas, I think the bar's on fire."

Patrick turned to look at where the old man was pointing and stared in shock at the flames. He caught sight of a figure rushing away from the bar, and he squinted, trying to make out who it was.

"There are people in there!" Harold yelled, pushing Patrick forward and breaking into a run towards the fire.

Patrick followed instantly, dazed from his shock, barely keeping up with the priest.

***

Jason Collick hurried away from the burning bar. He held his gun tight in his hand, almost tripping as he constantly looked over his shoulder. Black smoke escaped through the open door of the bar, rushing out in a large cloud and disappearing amidst the darkness. He could see the flames licking at the wooden interior, the fire inside raging out of control.

It had taken him a few seconds to respond to the fallen candle, the sawdust on the bar floor igniting almost immediately in a frenzy of flames. Jason had ignored the little man's wails, taking his gun from the bartender's belt and rushing out into the night where he thought he would be safe.

*Let them burn! Let them all burn!*

But he wasn't safe. The dead raced out, following him, their eyes set on Jason as he made his escape. He had hoped they couldn't leave the bar, that the flames would engulf them and rid him of their hollow stares and hissing voices. He would have no peace, though, and as he quickened his pace, the dead began to run towards him.

"Hey!"

Jason looked over his shoulder and almost screamed out as he saw Chuck rushing forward. The man was quick, neither affected by his wet suit nor the bullets in his chest. The side of his face that wasn't attached to the rest of his skull flapped in the wind as he raced forward, his smile crazed.

"Confess, Jason!" Chuck screamed into the night. "Confess!"

Terror-stricken, Jason tripped and fell hard onto the asphalt, watching in horror as Chuck advanced on him.

"Hey, man, stop!" Chuck yelled.

Jason raised his gun and fired.

\*\*\*

"The bar's on fire!"

Gina jumped up from the bed and raced to where Diana stood, holding the drapes aside as the flames danced across their reflections in the window.

Gina had tried her best to ignore the actress as she bitched and moaned about the power, happy that at least for the moment, the woman's attention was elsewhere. She only spoke up when Diana used her cellphone as a flashlight, reminding her that it would only kill her battery and there would be no way to recharge.

She hated how Diana had sneered at her, spitting more distasteful insults, but the fight was all out of Gina. She had her five minutes of glory. It was all she could muster for one night. She would let the actress win a few rounds for now.

Sal had finally woken up when Diana mentioned the fire, whispering something inaudible, but Gina's attention was elsewhere. She stood next to Diana in shock as they watched the flames burst through the bar windows, black smoke bellowing out. She could make out Owen and Connor lying on the ground in front of the flames, too close for comfort.

"Come on," Gina said, rushing towards the door.

"Where are you going?" Diana asked. "Are you out of your mind?"

Gina opened the door and stared at Diana in disbelief. "They need our help," she said, finding it hard to believe that she had to state the obvious.

"I'm not going anywhere," Diana replied.

Gina stared at her for a brief moment before they both flinched at the sudden sound of gunfire.

\*\*\*

Cameron heaved, his hands grasped tightly around Connor's arm as Owen pulled from the other. He could feel the strain of the bartender's weight against his back, and he only let go when they had dragged the man as far away from the fire as possible.

Cameron bent over, gasping for breath, coughing out the smoke that had infiltrated his lungs. Owen dropped onto the ground beside him and pointed frantically towards the pool.

"That bastard has his gun!" Owen stammered. "He has a gun, dammit!"

Cameron looked up and saw Jason Collick rushing away, halfway past the pool, towards the motel's second wing. He didn't think twice and immediately gave chase, pushing past the stinging pain in his chest.

"Hey!" he called out after Jason.

The man turned around, and seeing Cameron racing towards him, quickened his pace.

*Oh, no you don't!*

Cameron picked up speed, rushing forward through the wind that pushed back against him. From the corner of his eye, he imagined seeing a boy sitting on one of the lounge chairs beside the pool, watching him intently. Cameron shook the feeling away, his focus set on catching up with Jason.

"Hey, man, stop!"

Jason turned back again, and Cameron smiled when he watched him trip and fall.

*Now I got you.*

He saw the gun a few seconds too late.

\*\*\*

Patrick raced forward as soon as he saw the sparks erupt from the gun, followed by the deafening sounds of the gunshots. He could see Jason Collick clearly now, and Patrick yelled out in rage as Cameron Turk's body swirled and fell to the ground.

*He shot Cameron! The bastard actually shot him!*

Jason turned to Patrick and Harold, shifting his aim and firing again. Patrick felt a body slam against him just as a bullet grazed his shoulder, pain immediately bursting up and down his arm. He fell hard, Harold holding him down as they watched Jason jump to his feet and run towards the motel's second wing, the one Owen had told them was being renovated.

Patrick pushed Harold off him forcefully, fully intent on chasing the man to the far ends of hell if he had to, but Harold's old grasp was strong.

"Don't be stupid, Patrick!" Harold yelled. "Use your head! The man has a gun!"

Patrick struggled against Harold's grip, but the priest was stronger than he had imagined, pinning him down and keeping him as immobile as possible. Gina raced out from behind the corner, kicking off her heels as she fell to her knees beside Cameron's still body. He watched as she shook at him, calling out his name over and over again, more frantically each time. There was no response from Cameron.

Patrick cried out in rage. Looking past Gina, he caught sight of a young boy sitting cross-legged on a pool lounge, staring out at them from within the shadows.

Jimmy Frey stood up slowly, walked in the opposite direction of the pool and disappeared.

## Chapter 13

"You can't just leave!"

Gina Andrews lowered her eyes and sighed, grabbing a few more clothes from her closet and folding them softly into her small suitcase. Her mother watched her angrily, her eyes blazing and her hands on her hips, infuriated by Gina's lack of response.

"You have responsibilities!" she said. "You leave no one in charge, and everything collapses."

"Mother, that's not true," Gina said, avoiding the older woman's gaze. "I'm leaving you in charge."

"And who says I want this?"

Gina almost broke out laughing. Ever since the company had made its first million, her mother had wanted to push her to the sidelines and take over. Gina made it a point not to give the woman too much power, making sure she was responsible for enough to keep her content, but not to make any serious changes. For years, she could see it in the older woman's eyes; she wanted the company. She actually believed that she deserved it.

"I'm sorry, mother," Gina said. "I'm going to have to burden you with it all for just a few days. I'll be back by Monday."

Her mother sighed and looked up, faking her frustration. "Fine, I'll do what I can. It's not like I have the ability to be of any real use."

Gina glanced at her mother and then turned away, unable to meet the woman's eyes for too long. She couldn't help it; her mother intimidated her.

"It's procedural stuff," Gina said. "The new launch isn't for another four weeks, so don't worry, you won't be hassled by it all."

"Actually," her mother cut in. "I had a few ideas for that."

"I'm sure you do," Gina muttered.

"Excuse me?"

Gina looked up at her mother and smiled, her face turning a bright red. "Nothing, mother," she said quickly. "We can talk about it when I get back."

"Or I can get it done while you're away and save us some time."

"I thought you didn't want the burdens of running the company," Gina said.

"Well, if I'm going to have to do it anyway."

"It's okay," Gina said, giving her mother the best reassuring smile she could muster. "I'll be back before you know it and we'll have enough time to discuss whatever you need."

Her mother's frown deepened, and Gina quickly turned away, knowing that she would never hear the end of this. It didn't matter, though. She needed to get as far away from all this as possible, particularly her mother. Any more push, and she might just give in to her mother's wishes, and she knew that would only end in a disaster.

"At least tell me where you're going," her mother cut through her thoughts.

"I'm not sure, yet," Gina said. "You can reach me on my cellphone."

Her mother puffed. "Typical," she said. "Your father did the same thing all the time. It's disgusting how alike the two of you are."

Gina froze, the mention of her father always a sore point in their conversation. For ten years now, her mother still wasn't tired of bringing it up whenever she thought it would hurt Gina the most. It was one of the things she hated about the woman.

"Then again, you *are* daddy's little girl, aren't you?" her mother sneered.

Gina felt tears well up in her eyes and quickly brushed them away. She looked at her mother angrily and pointed to the door.

"Get out," Gina whispered.

"What did you say to me?" her mother frowned.

"Get out!" Gina screamed. "Get out, get out, get out!"

The older woman's eyes widened in shock at her daughter's sudden outburst, and without another word, she hurried out of the room.

Gina slammed her suitcase shut, sat down heavily on the side of her bed, and burst into tears.

\*\*\*

Patrick pounded his fist against the door to room 219.

He was enraged. So many things were happening at the same time, so much inexplicable incidents one after the other, that he feared he was going completely insane. He felt like he could handle the consistent night and rain, and maybe even come to some kind of terms with the fact that no one could actually leave the motel. But now a man was dead, and a second dying, and the entirety of the world around him that just yesterday had made complete sense was slowly falling apart.

Patrick wanted answers, and he knew exactly where to find them.

He pounded on the door again, catching the sound of a quick shuffling of feet as someone moved inside. He tried to look through the window by the door, but the drapes were drawn. Frustrated, he kicked at the door several times before it finally opened.

Tara Frey stared out at him from the darkness of the room, her hair perfectly framing her face, her gaze serious. She did not look like a woman who took kindly to intrusions, her eyes fixed sternly on him, but Patrick couldn't care less.

"Where's your son?" Patrick asked, teeth clenched in rage, his fists shaking.

Tara was just an inch or two shorter than him, and with the door only slightly open, she blocked any chance of looking past her and into the room. He stared her down threateningly, almost as if he could move her out of the way with just his gaze.

Tara didn't reply.

"Where is your son?" Patrick asked again, slower, stressing on each word that came out of his mouth.

Tara cocked her head to one side. "What do you want from him?"

Patrick took deep breaths, knowing that if the woman stalled any longer, he might just hit her. Right now, he was on autopilot, driven entirely by emotion, logic thrown out the window completely.

"Answers," Patrick hissed. "He knows what's going on in this damned motel, and he is going to tell me everything, or I swear to you, I'll have everyone crashing into this room and pulling the both of you out by your hair."

Tara smiled, amused by Patrick's misplaced confidence. "Mr. Lahm, I don't believe you'll find what you're looking for here."

Patrick lost all control and rushed forward, pushing past her into the darkness. He found Jimmy sitting next to the window, watching him intently, in much the same way he had seen him sitting at the pool. Patrick made for the boy, but before he could get within a few feet, he felt a strong hand grab him by the arm and twist painfully.

Patrick cried out as he dropped to one knee, looking up at his attacker, slightly confused as to how comfortable she looked while pinning him down. He tried to break free of her hold, but that only made things worse as something clicked in his elbow and fire shot up his arm.

"You're hurting him," Jimmy said softly, his eyes fixated on Patrick as the man squirmed under Tara's grip.

"Believe me, I'd do the same to her if I had the chance," Patrick said, trying to remain completely still, unwilling to endure any more pain.

"She's a little protective," Jimmy smiled. The boy got up, walked past Patrick and closed the door. He switched on a lamp on his way back, and Patrick closed his eyes against the sudden brightness.

"We should remain in the dark," Tara said to her son.

Jimmy shrugged. "No one can see us. They're all in the manager's apartment."

"How do you have power?" Patrick asked, looking from Jimmy to Tara and back again.

"This place is untainted," Tara replied, slightly loosening her grip and raising an eyebrow questioningly.

Patrick nodded, assuring her he would behave, and she let go of his arm.

"Rules bend here," Jimmy said with a smile, returning to his seat.

Patrick flexed and extended his arm, loosening the knots in his muscles and shaking the pain away.

"You were at the pool," he said to Jimmy.

Jimmy nodded. "I was."

"You saw what happened," Patrick continued. "Did you know?"

Jimmy nodded again.

"Why didn't you warn us?" Patrick's voice rose. "You didn't even try to stop it!"

"He's thirteen," Tara said, crossing the room and sitting on the bed. "What was he supposed to do?" She crossed her legs, closed her eyes and lowered her head.

"He could have said something to any of us," Patrick said. He turned back to Jimmy. "How did you know? How could you possibly know?"

Jimmy glanced at his mother, checking for any kind of reaction, and when it seemed like she would not protest, he sighed and unfolded his legs. He slid off his seat and sat down in front of Patrick, staring directly in his eyes.

"I know things," Jimmy said. "Things people shouldn't know. Things that I wish I never knew."

Patrick frowned. "Like the rain?"

Jimmy nodded. "And the spiders."

Patrick felt his heart jump. "How do you know about the spiders?"

"I know you hear voices, that your dreams are disturbed, that you're plagued by your sins," Jimmy replied. "It's the same with everyone else here. It's the reason why all this is happening."

Patrick sat frozen in place, gazing at the boy in disbelief. He felt like he was in a dream again, and in a few seconds he would see spiders crawl out of Jimmy's orifices and make their way towards him, promising to swallow him whole. He would wake up, screaming, and all would be as it was. Harold would be at the bar, Cameron would be alive, and the rain would still be falling.

Jimmy gave him a sad smile and shook his head. "You're not dreaming."

Patrick opened his mouth to reply, but nothing came out. He was at a loss for words, helpless to make any sense of his situation. He felt like he was back in the void, lost in its murky nothingness, unable to breathe. The world was closing in around him, suffocating him, a strong sense of claustrophobia engulfed him.

"You're losing him," Tara said from the bed. "Maybe he's not as strong as you thought he was."

Patrick blinked and shook his head. He turned to find the woman staring directly at him, watching him as a scientist would observe a test subject, waiting for the desired results. All she needed was a lab coat and clipboard, and Patrick could safely say he had gone completely mad. That all this, the motel, the book signing, the spiders, everything, was just in his head. It was the only logical explanation. He had gone crazy and was hallucinating.

Jimmy snapped his fingers. "Stay with me, Mr. Lahm," the boy said.

"I'm sorry," Patrick frowned, feeling the beginnings of a migraine manifest itself. "I'm a little confused."

"I know," Jimmy said. "This was quite a shock for me, too. Luckily, my mother was around to help me through it."

"Through what?"

Jimmy sighed and looked at his mother for assurance, and the woman nodded at him.

"The sins," Jimmy said. "Everyone has them, and they hang about a person like an ugly black cloud. You don't see them, nobody does, but you can feel them. The guilt, the fear, the what-if's. They rule you, push you in directions you would have otherwise never thought of taking. They dig their way deep into your soul until they become a part of you that you can never rid yourself of."

"You can see that?"

Jimmy nodded. "And a lot more. I can see how black it turns a person's soul, and when that darkness becomes heavy, when you can lose yourself in it, *they* come for you."

"Who are *they*?"

"Soul collectors," Tara spoke up. "They find the darkest of us, the ones with the greatest sins, and they come for us. They bring your sins to life, manifest them in ways that could drive a person insane, or worse."

Patrick shook his head quickly, knowing that there was no sensible explanation to anything he was hearing. "I've never heard of anything like that before."

Jimmy smiled. "There are a lot of things out there people have never heard of before," he said. "It doesn't mean they aren't there."

"And you think the man who killed Cameron is one of these, what do you call them?"

"Soul collectors," Jimmy replied. "We're not sure. It's why I couldn't say anything."

Patrick looked at Tara for confirmation, but the woman's eyes were closed again. She looked like she was meditating, but her mouth was moving, soft whispers filling the room. Patrick tried to make out what she was saying, but the language was foreign to him.

"The truth is, soul collectors possess their victims, so it's not always easy to spot them. Jason Collick might just be haunted by his sins. I'm not sure if he's confessed yet."

Patrick's head turned quickly to the boy. "What did you say?"

"Confession," Jimmy replied. "It's how they possess your body. When you confess."

A loud clap of thunder startled Patrick, and he looked out the window as rain fell in sheets, sudden and without warning.

Tara's eyes opened. "It's starting again."

\*\*\*

Gina's cellphone rang.

"You have a working phone?" Diana asked, startled by the sound.

113

Gina looked at her, then to the others. Heat rose to her cheeks. She was very uncomfortable with being the center of attention. The night was taking a toll on her, and she was extremely exhausted. She didn't need the extra burden of having to explain why her phone only seemed to work when her mother wanted to call her. She quickly pulled her cellphone out, cancelled, and set it to airplane mode.

"It's an alarm," she lied, holding up her phone to show her audience the empty bars.

Her comment had the desired effect, with most of the guests returning to what they had been doing before the shrill sound of the ringing broke the uncomfortable silence. Diana, however, was squinting at her in disbelief. Gina avoided the other woman's gaze and quickly left the small apartment, stepping out into the cold night and walking as far away from earshot as possible.

Gina looked back to make sure no one was following her, and took her cellphone out again. Before she could do anything, it began to ring again, and she cried out and dropped it. Her mother's name flashed on the screen, a menacing reminder that no matter what Gina did, the older woman would continue to harass her until she answered.

Gina bent down and retrieved her phone, noticing that it was still on airplane mode, and looked over her shoulder again at the apartment. Diana was watching her through the window, and Gina quickly pocketed the phone and walked further away towards the pool. She passed through the gates and sat down heavily on a lounge chair, staring dumbfounded at her screen as it flashed, urging her to act.

"Hello?" Gina finally answered.

"Where the hell have you been?" her mother screamed from the other line. "I've been trying to reach you for days!"

Gina winced at the shrill sound of the other woman, a rude reminder of why she had been ignoring the calls and how answering her phone was a big mistake.

"Mother, it's barely been a day," Gina said.

"A day!" her mother yelled. "Are you high again? Where are you?"

Gina looked about the dark motel and towards the burnt-down bar. "Just outside Hartford, at a motel."

"Good," her mother said. "Get in your car and drive back here immediately. You should be back by dusk,"

Gina frowned and looked at the time on her phone, the digital numbers telling her it was still midnight. What was her mother talking about?

"Are you listening to me?"

Gina replaced her phone on her ear. "What time is it?" she asked.

Her mother sighed, clearly irritated by her daughter's question. "What have you been smoking, Gina?"

"Nothing!" Gina's voice rose, echoing through the dark. She could almost sense her mother flinch on the other line. Gina quickly calmed herself down. "Nothing, mother, I haven't been smoking. Just tell me what time it is."

"It's ten in the morning," her mother answered, clearly unhappy that she had been yelled out, her tone ringing promises of reprisal. "We have a lot of problems here, and I expect you back today."

"Ten in the morning?" Gina asked.

"Listen to me, you spoilt cow," her mother suddenly hissed. "I don't care if you're on another one of your pitiful bouts of depression, or if you're going cross-country and sleeping with every homeless idiot willing to disregard your ugly mounds and stick it to you anyway. For all I care, you can whore yourself to an entire biker gang until they screw the fat off you! But you will do as I say, Gina Dolores Andrews, or I will find you and bring you back in pieces."

Gina felt her mother's words hit her like a punch to the gut, her eyes wide, her hands shaking as she took it all in. Only, it didn't sound like her mother. The woman's voice changed, became much deeper, angrier, spitting her horrid words in pure disgust. She had never talked to Gina in that way before, although her eyes had usually portrayed what she was thinking. Gina knew her mother had no love for her, not since high school anyway, and she was finally voicing her true feelings.

"What? Surprised?" her mother sneered. "I know what you really are. You don't deserve your success or your money, or the fancy clothes you wear to hide the ugliness inside you. Do you think I don't know? Do you think *he* never told me?"

Gina's body shook uncontrollably, her mind urging her to hang up now before the conversation grew any uglier, but she couldn't do it. A part of her believed that even if she did hang up, she would still be able to hear her mother.

"I know everything, Gina, and one day I'm going to make you pay for what you did. I'm going to make you squirm at my feet when I take everything away from you."

"Mother, I ..."

"Don't you 'mother' me!" the older woman screamed, and Gina dropped her phone.

She hugged herself and began to rock back and forth, crying freely now, her mind spinning with what she had heard, her mother's voice still screaming from the cellphone on the ground.

"Confess!" Gina heard her mother screaming. "Confess your sins, you little bitch!"

Gina kicked her phone into the pool.

***

"Confess!"

Sal opened his eyes, his lids heavy. He hurt everywhere, the pain cutting at every part of his body. He could feel the heat coursing through him, numbing him, yet not enough to mask the agony he was going through. He turned his head slightly to one side and looked out at his room.

"Confess!"

The voice was close, but even with his eyes open, his vision was blurry and Sal couldn't make out where the sound was coming from. The room was dark except for the moonlight coming through the large window, creating shadows everywhere. Sal knew he was probably imagining the voice, a byproduct of his fever, but it was far too clear for comfort.

"Oh, Sal, look at what he's done to you."

Sal recognized the voice and felt a sudden pain in his chest, his heartbeat quickening. He pushed himself up, feeling about until he found the side of the bed and rolled into a sitting position.

"Mrs. Little?" Sal stammered.

A woman sat on the chair opposite him, half-hidden in the shadows, her figure only a silhouette in the dark. But he would have recognized those shoes anywhere, black flats with pink flowers drawn on the sides, the shoes they had buried her in. He remembered commenting to Connor about them, that it was a shame to throw away good shoes like that. He could still feel Connor's eyes boring into him disapprovingly.

"How are you, Sal?"

Sal closed his eyes and opened them again.

*This isn't right.*

Convinced that he was hallucinating, Sal tried to stand up, his legs weak and shaking, holding the edge of the bed to keep his balance. He felt a burst of blood rush out of his leg where the bone was still extruded, and for some strange reason, the pain had disappeared completely.

He looked at the woman and shuddered. It was definitely Mrs. Little, although her voice did seem a little raspier, as if she were talking with sand in her mouth.

*Or dirt. Did you ever think of that, Sal? She probably ate her way out of her grave.*

"So he got to you, too, did he?" Mrs. Little giggled. "I thought he would. He wouldn't let you live very long with a secret like that."

Sal froze as the woman stood up and stepped out of the shadow, slowly, legs shuffling against the carpet as if she were dragging her weight forward. What was left of the woman who once ran this motel gave him a toothless smile, her skin grey and peeling, her head littered with stray strands of what was left of her hair. From her left ear hung a single diamond earring, her other earlobe ripped where Sal had stolen the second one just before tossing the first shovels of dirt on her coffin.

All that didn't bother him as much as her eyes. Her pale blue eyes, ice cold, gazing at him with a look that promised pain and suffering for all eternity. Sal could see past the icy stare to the pits of hell through those eyes, and he suddenly felt the temperature in the room drop dangerously.

"Confess!" Mrs. Little smiled. "Confess, Sal!"

Sal shook his head in a daze, praying for the hallucinations to disappear. He moved slowly to one side as Mrs. Little approached him, the shuffling of her feet loud in the dark room.

"Confess!"

Sal felt himself swoon and he quickly grabbed onto the commode to stop his fall. He looked towards the door, now too far away and blocked by the monster that was once his boss. Mrs. Little laughed, and Sal felt the sound cut through his mind like razors.

"Why did you do it, Sal?" Mrs. Little asked. "Did you think he'd take you in? Did you think my husband would be so grateful for your loyalty, that he would let you run things around here?"

Mrs. Little shuffled forward, forcing Sal to limp further away. He was losing a lot of blood despite the make-shift tourniquet around his thigh. The fact that there was no pain worried him, and he wondered if maybe he was going into shock.

Sal looked at his bloody leg, then back up, and cried out when Mrs. Little grabbed him by the back of his neck and propelled him into the bathroom. Sal felt light, as if he were being carried off his feet, until he was standing directly in front of the mirror above the sink, staring at his reflection and the dead face of Mrs. Little behind him.

"Look at yourself, Sal," she hissed in his ear. "Look at what's become of you."

Sal stared into his haggard face, his eyes sunken, his cheekbones prominent against his sickly visage. He was sweating profusely, and he tasted blood as it trickled out of his mouth and down his chin.

"Confess," Mrs. Little whispered. "Confess, and it will all be over."

Sal whimpered, shaking his head slowly, the nape of his neck like ice under her grip. "It's not my fault," he coughed, his voice hoarse and his tongue heavy.

Mrs. Little smiled, a terrifying curl of the lips that left little to the imagination of what her intentions were. "That's where you're wrong, Sal," she said. "That's where you're terribly wrong."

Sal's head was thrust forward, and he screamed as his face slammed into the mirror again and again.

## Chapter 14

Patrick raced down the stairs at the sound of Sal's screaming, Tara close behind him. He took the steps by twos, heart pounding, the man's screams a terrifying sound in the otherwise quiet motel. He had no idea what to expect, but with Tara following him and keeping up, he could assume the worst.

Patrick burst into Sal's room, throwing his weight against the door when it wouldn't open at first, and tried the lights. Whatever was giving the Freys their power was obviously not at work here, but Patrick didn't need light to see what was happening.

Sal was standing in front of the bathroom mirror, his hands clenching the sink tight, his injured leg bent awkwardly as blood poured out in dark streaks that formed a large puddle beneath him. Sal was slamming his face against the broken mirror, the shards that were still in place tearing at his face as he screamed.

Patrick raced towards him, but was stopped abruptly by Tara.

"No!" she yelled over the other man's screams.

Patrick pulled away from her, rushing towards Sal just as the other man stopped moving and fell in a heap to the floor. Patrick fell down next to him, grimacing at the sheer amount of blood around him, trying to decide what to do first.

"Sal!" Patrick yelled. "Jesus, man, what were you thinking?"

Sal's eyes stared out into nothing, parts of his cheek and forehead hanging loose, the bones beneath clearly visible. Patrick felt for a pulse, and when he found none, pushed himself away from the dead body and against the bathroom wall. His body shook uncontrollably, and try as he could, he couldn't take his eyes off Sal.

Tara walked into the bathroom and bent down to one knee next to the body, mimicking Patrick as she made sure Sal was dead.

"What was that?" Patrick stammered. "What would drive a man to do that?"

Tara looked at him, the expression on her face one of exhaustion and sadness. "It will only get worse from here on out," she said. "We need to find the others."

\*\*\*

Jason Collick sat in the dark, knees drawn up to his chest, surrounded by the dead.

They were never going to let him go. He knew that now. They were everywhere, taunting him, screaming at him, tearing at him until he could no longer differentiate what was real and what wasn't. Their voices echoed in his head, even when they weren't speaking to him, and there was nothing he could do about it.

He couldn't kill them, and he couldn't run away from them. That much was obvious. He had seen Chuck fall. He had shot the man and had seen him crumble to the pavement. Yet, his ex-partner now stood across the empty room, staring at Jason angrily, waiting. Jason had no idea what the man was waiting for, but it didn't matter. There was nothing he could do to stop what was coming.

"Confess," Chuck whispered from across the room.

Jason looked up at him, and quickly took in the gazes of the rest of the dead around him. They had grown silent, their pale faces emotionless now as they stared at him, patiently waiting for his response. Chuck coughed violently, bent over and vomited a stream of blood and water.

Jason watched him wipe his mouth and stand up straight again, smiling. "Confess, Jason," the man managed to sputter.

Jason sniffed and dropped his eyes to the gun in his hands. He raised it lazily and fired, watching the drywall behind Chuck burst into pieces of plaster.

*You can't kill him.*

Jason's arm dropped and his head rolled back. He was tired, exhausted to the point that he couldn't make sense of anything that was happening. There was barely any light seeping through the bare window. The room he sat in, one of the many waiting to be refurbished for business, was desolate, and Jason contemplated lying down and trying to sleep.

"There will be no rest for the wicked," a voice rang in his ears, and Jason gazed lazily at a little girl sitting to one side on the frame of a broken chair, her dark eyes fixated on him as she swung her legs back and forth.

"I'm not wicked," Jason protested, his voice barely audible, his tongue rolling.

Chuck moved away from the wall and trudged forward, Jason watching him come. He would not fight anymore. He was too tired. He didn't care what Chuck or the other dead would do to him; he just wanted it to be over.

Chuck hunched down in front of him and grabbed his jaw, his fingers cold. "Confess, Jason," he said. "Confess and it will end now."

Jason gazed into the dead man's eyes and remembered the hatred he had always felt towards him. He remembered how Chuck had always stolen the limelight, had become the center of attention and the figure everyone sought out for leadership. The man had always stood in Jason's way, shutting down all his ideas, making him look like a fool in front of his employees. Chuck had wanted it all, had wanted to keep pushing Jason to one side until he was obsolete, just a founder's name people would quickly forget.

Jason hated him. He leaned forward, forcefully pushing against Chuck's grip, and looked the dead man in the eye. "I killed you," Jason spat.

Chuck smiled and let go of Jason.

"I wanted you dead the minute you'd grown too big for the both of us," Jason continued. "I waited for the right moment and I pulled the trigger. I dropped your body in the river. I lied to the faces of every living soul, pinned the murder on your drunk brother, and laughed through it all. I did it. Is that what you want to hear? I did it!"

Chuck stood up and nodded, smiling as he stepped back and raised his arms to the dead sitting around them.

"I faked numbers, ruined lives, fired the dead weight to increase my profits, and tore apart the lives of those who dared to sue!" Jason yelled out to the rest of the room. "I'm responsible for your bankruptcy, for your suicides, for your spiral into alcoholism and drugs. I ruined the future of your children, broke apart your marriages, and screwed you all."

The dead all stood up, one by one, their faces suddenly relaxed as they watched Jason confess.

"And you want to know something?" Jason hissed. "I'd do it all again!"

Chuck began to laugh. Jason watched as the soft chuckle slowly grew into a manic shriek that rang through the room and across the motel. Suddenly, everything seemed much clearer, the curtain in front of his eyes lifting as the world around him made perfect sense. Jason knew what was expected of him, and his grip tightened around his gun.

Chuck continued to laugh, and Jason laughed along with him.

\*\*\*

Patrick was in Owen's apartment with the other guests when the gunshot startled them all.

"We have to find him," Harold said, voicing what everyone else was thinking. "There's no telling what he will do."

Patrick was about to reply when Connor interrupted him.

"I'm sorry, but what do you mean you couldn't leave?"

The burly man sat on the couch furthest away from the others, Harold having had suggested to give him enough space to come to. They had filled him in on everything that had happened, and Connor was not in the least bit happy. The bar was his home, and seeing it black with soot and crumbling from the fire angered him tremendously.

Now he was listening to Patrick tell them that Sal was dead, and a part of him wanted to rush across the motel, find Jason Collick, and smash his head in with a flat iron.

"That doesn't matter right now," Patrick said, "and it's going to take a while to explain." He ventured a glance at Tara standing near one wall, watching them closely. He wondered if leaving Jimmy alone in the room was a good idea.

"What matters is stopping Jason before anything else happens," Patrick said. "I think he's behind what's going on here."

"What *is* going on here?" Diana asked.

"I'm not exactly sure," Patrick said.

"Then why do you think that maniac out there is the reason for anything?" the actress asked. "I mean, it's terrible what happened to Sal, but from what you said, it sounds more like the man was a complete psycho."

"Hey, watch it," Owen spat. "That man was my friend."

Connor scoffed and looked away when Owen gazed at him.

"Whatever," Diana said. "Listen, I don't know what you guys are getting at, but I'm going to stay here and wait until the sun comes up, then I'm walking the hell out of this place."

"The sun isn't coming up any time soon," Tara said.

Diana turned to her angrily. "Listen, miss dark-and-brooding, I don't know you, and I really don't care, but you're kind of ruining the little bit of positive energy I still have, okay?"

"Shut up, Diana," Gina mumbled.

Patrick looked at the woman sitting in front of the window, staring out at into the rainy night. She had been quiet ever since he and Tara had walked in and told them about Sal.

"What did you say to me?" Diana hissed.

"You heard me," Gina replied, unmoving.

Diana got up quickly. "I have half the mind to—"

Kurt immediately grabbed her and sat her back down, his hands on her shoulders pinning her in her seat. Diana tried to shake herself free, but Kurt's hold was strong, and she looked up at him angrily.

"Let go of me," she threatened.

"We have bigger things to worry about, missy," he said, looking at her calmly. "Why don't you postpone your squabbles for later?"

Diana huffed and tried to break free again, with less enthusiasm this time, before finally sitting still.

Kurt returned his attention to Patrick. "I have a shotgun in the car," he said matter-of-factly. "There's another gun in the glove compartment that you can use."

"I've never used a gun before," Patrick admitted, pushing past his initial desire to shoot down Kurt's obvious suggestion and look for a more amiable solution. He couldn't deny that

Jason was dangerous, and they already had a dead body to prove it. Kurt was obviously not going to wait for someone else to join Cameron and Sal.

"Are the two of you out of your minds?" Owen cut in. "This isn't the wild west. You can't go around shooting up the place!"

"I have a rifle in my room," Connor said, standing up. He ignored Owen's gaze. "I'll get it and meet you guys by the pool."

"Are you sure this is a good idea?" Harold asked. "Surely there must be another way."

Patrick placed a hand on the priest's shoulder and squeezed. "We're just going to bring him in," Patrick said. "We're not going to kill him."

"Speak for yourself," Connor said.

"Are you sure you're rested enough for this?" Patrick asked, ignoring the man's previous comment and hoping he wouldn't have to subdue two gun-toting maniacs.

Connor waved at him. "Don't worry about me," he said, making his way to the door. "It's going to take more than a blow to the head to slow me down. Besides, the other wing of the motel is bigger. You're going to need the extra hands."

Connor stepped out into the rain and closed the door behind him.

Harold gave Patrick a worried look. "I don't see this ending very well," he said.

Patrick couldn't reply.

## Chapter 15

Jimmy watched the rain from under the protection of the second floor landing. The storm had picked up tremendously, the winds swirling the rain about, the temperature low and chilling. It worried Jimmy greatly, and despite his promise to stay put, he knew that his mother alone would not be able to handle the soul collector if they came face to face with it.

*Not if. When.*

Jimmy knew it to be true. He could sense it in ever part of his body; Jason Collick had confessed, and was now nothing more than a puppet for the real monster. He could see Patrick and Kurt standing near the pool with their guns, and could hear Connor's footsteps below as the big man made his way back to them. They believed they were ready, although Jimmy knew that each one of them was as vulnerable as Jason had been.

The soul collector would fight back. It had its first victim. There would be no more games; the monster was going to go for the kill. Jimmy only hoped that Patrick and the others would be able to bring it down before it turned everyone in the motel on each other.

Jimmy looked past the men and to the trees behind the pool. He caught sight of his mother rushing between the foliage, slipping past Patrick and the others on her way towards the other side of the motel. Jimmy's heart dropped, knowing what she intended to do. He contemplated calling out to Patrick, but knew that would only make things worse. They needed to focus on the task at hand, not rushing in after his mother.

Jimmy made up his mind quickly, abandoning the shelter of the second floor landing and racing downstairs and into the rain. In the dark, he rushed across the motel to the second wing.

*** 

"They're coming for you."

Jason no longer saw the dead, alone in the dark room with his gun pressed to his forehead. His eyes were closed, Chuck's voice only whispered echoes in his head. He could see them, though. He could see the three men standing outside, talking amongst each, stealing glance at the second wing as they made their plans.

They would not find him easily, and when they did, he would be ready. He would have the upper hand. Jason opened his eyes, ejected his gun's magazine and counted four bullets. He smiled to himself.

Four would be enough.

***

"So we're good here?"

Connor checked his rifle before slapping it and nodding, the scowl on his face deep. Patrick knew the man was angry, and could only imagine what he would do to Jason Collick once they found him. There was a silent agreement between them all that they would try to unarm Jason and bring him in, but Patrick doubted Connor would wait very long before firing a round or two into the maniac.

"You okay?" he asked Connor.

"The second wing has an extra twenty rooms," Connor explained, ignoring the question as rain seeped into his eyes. "Basically, what you see from here are the rooms looking out at the parking lot. There's a second set behind them, and a corridor in between both rows."

"But we can rule out those ten," Kurt said, pointing with his gun.

Connor shook his head. "The rooms on the outside have a second door to the corridor," he said. "We might not have seen him go into any of them from here, but there's no saying he didn't go in from the back."

"Why would you have two doors into one room?" Kurt asked. "Whose idea was that?"

"Mrs. Little," Connor said. "Before she died, she really wanted to spice this place up. Spent a fortune on that second wing, making the rooms bigger and all. The idea was turning the second landing into a balcony." Connor looked back over his shoulder at Owen's apartment. "Her husband never followed through."

"So what's the plan?" Kurt looked to Patrick.

Patrick had no idea. He had never done anything like this before, his only experience stemming from movies he watched and strategy games on his son's computer. This was way over his head, and he would have traded in his leadership of the situation to anyone else if he could. The two men looked at him questioningly, and he could see in their eyes that they trusted him fully, relying on him to guide them through what they had to do.

Patrick felt the burden heavy on his shoulders.

"Go in from the side," Patrick finally suggested. "Do the back rooms have a landing as well?"

Connor shook his head. "Just the corridor and that one there."

"How good are you with that thing?" Patrick gestured to the rifle.

"Good enough."

"Ok, so you keep your eyes on the landing outside while Kurt and I take the corridor," Patrick said. "That way, if he tries to get out from there, you'll spot him."

"And if he runs?" Kurt asked.

"There's nowhere to run to," Connor replied, the look in his eyes portraying exactly what he intended to do if Jason did decide to flee.

Patrick didn't like the look at all.

"Pretty straightforward," Kurt muttered, hunching his shoulders. "After you, boss."

Patrick nodded and led the way.

\*\*\*

Gina heard singing.

It was low, barely audible in the frantic chatter going on around her, but Gina heard it clearly. She recognized the song, too. It was an old tune her father used to sing to her when she was a child, the same one he had sung in the shower while she lay curled up naked in her bed, guilty over what she had just done.

The singing made her shudder.

Gina looked around at the others. Harold was arguing with Diana about something, and Owen had excused himself minutes before and disappeared into his bedroom. There was no sign that anyone heard the singing besides her, and she turned her gaze back to the window.

Someone was outside, walking in the rain to a small structure Owen had told them was where the generators were stored. Gina could tell it was a woman, and only then noticed that Tara was not in the room either.

*What is she doing? She shouldn't be outside.*

Gina stood up quickly, grabbed her coat, and exited the room unnoticed, rushing after Tara.

***

They made their way up the flight of stairs slowly, guns lowered, eyes searching for any movement inside the rooms. The windows were bare, one of the many things Patrick would eventually be grateful for, and a few of the doors hung limply on their hinges. He glanced at Connor who nodded to him and immediately broke away from the group.

Kurt and Patrick moved to the left, checking the first room facing the pool quickly before cautiously making their way into the corridor.

"Looks like a bad dream," Kurt said, and Patrick couldn't agree more.

The corridor was dark, extending narrowly down the entire length of the wing. Patrick immediately felt claustrophobic, unwilling to step any further, his eyes suddenly watering as he imagined the walls shutting closed on him once he was between them.

Wire hung loose from the ceiling, the floors littered with broken plaster and buckets of paint. Something moved under a few cardboard boxes a few yards in front of them, and Patrick felt dread race through him as he imagined black little spiders crawling out. A rat bolted from its hiding place and raced into one of the open doors, and Patrick let out a long sigh of relief.

They moved forward, Kurt a few feet ahead, peeking into the rooms to his left as Patrick searched the ones on the right. He could see Connor through the windows, the man briefly giving him a wave before continuing forward, and Patrick felt his tense muscles ease. Between the three of them, he didn't see how Jason would be able to slip by unnoticed.

*** 

"Confess!"

Owen Little sat up in a start.

He had excused himself from the rest of the group, hoping to get a little shut eye before any more unwanted excitement, and had been halfway into a dreamless slumber when the voice pulled him back. He was alone, the room dark except for the small light from his cellphone. He could hear muffled shouting coming from behind the closed door, the angry sounds of Harold Bell against Diana's annoying whining.

"You think too much," a voice whispered from the shadows. "That was always your problem."

A figure stepped out from the darkness, skin loose, eyes hollow and only half a head of hair. Owen stared at his dead wife in horror, having had convinced himself that he had only imagined her in the truck before. Now she stood tall in front of him, smiling from across the room, her eyes blazing. Blood dripped onto the carpet from her hands, and he could make out strands of grey hair clutched in her fists; hair that looked vaguely like Sal's.

"Oh yes, Sal and I had a nice conversation," his wife said, coughing a raspy chuckle. "He adored you, worshipped you even, and now look what happened to him."

Owen scrambled from the bed, rolling onto the floor and rushing for the door. His wife grabbed him by the arm, ridiculously faster than he was and much stronger, pulling him back and hurtling him against the bed.

"In a way," she hissed, "his death is on your hands. Poor man couldn't take the pressure."

"Stay away from me!" Owen shouted, pushing away from his wife, raising his voice loud enough for the others outside to hear him. He called out to them, but that only made his wife laugh, and she lunged forward.

Owen felt her cold hands wrap around his neck just as she slammed his head against the wall, her thumbs suddenly pressing down on his windpipe as he tried to scream out for help. He gazed into her eyes in horror, her smile a toothless void of rotten flesh, the stench coming from her unbearable. Owen punched out at her, trying to breathe against her vice-like grip, but she was too strong.

Owen's vision began to blur, and he slowly fell into a perpetual darkness with only the sound of his dead wife's laughter ringing in his ears.

\*\*\*

The singing was louder.

Gina could hear it clearly as she made her way into the generator room, slowly and carefully, pushing the door all the way open and wincing as its hinges creaked. A single bulb hung from the ceiling, swaying slightly against the wind that blew in through the door, casting shadows of different shapes and sizes in its wake. Gina frowned as she gazed upwards, unable to comprehend how there was power here when the rest of the motel was in complete darkness.

*Why are you so surprised? Nobody's phone works except for yours, right?*

At least it did before she had kicked it into the pool. Gina shook her head and continued forward. She made her way between two large shelving units that created a makeshift corridor, boxes framing her in and making it impossible to see who was singing on the other side of the barricade.

Gina caught herself mouthing the words along with the tune, an instinct of hers since she was a little girl. She had loved that song, and had always looked forward to the nights her father would come home early and sing it to her. Now the tune made her skin crawl and her stomach turn, its sentimental memory ruined by one dreadful mistake.

There was no sign of Tara anywhere, and Gina slowly rounded the line of shelves and stepped into the small vestibule where three large generators sat idly side by side. Gina's eyes quickly found the source of the singing, a woman standing in front of a table to one side with her back to her. Gina instantly recognized her, and although she wanted to turn and run for the door, escape back into the rain and cold night, she found herself inexplicably frozen in place.

Her mother turned around and winked at her. "There you are," she said, her voice hard and angry despite the smile on her face. "I knew you'd find me."

Gina shuddered as she met her mother's gaze, her mind racing as it tried to make sense of what she was seeing. Her mother raised a finger and shook it slowly, side to side, pouting as she eyed her daughter.

"Now, it's about time we had that little talk," the older woman said, her face cracking and shifting. "Isn't that right, dear?"

Gina finally found her voice and screamed.

***

Patrick froze, his hand reaching out and grabbing Kurt instinctively.

The sound of screaming pierced through the night, loud despite the thunderous noise of the storm. His hand clenched tight on his gun, and he looked through the room to his right at Connor.

"That can't be good," Kurt said.

Patrick cursed out loud. A part of him was sure that Jason was still in the second wing, that there was some other explanation for the screaming they were hearing. Then again, he could have been wrong, and maybe the lunatic had found some way to circle around them and get to the others. Patrick glanced back down the length of the corridor.

*No. He's here. I can feel it.*

Patrick glanced at the other two men staring at him, waiting for him to tell them what to do. Patrick could sense the urgency in their eyes, and knew he had to make a decision now. He wanted to keep moving forward, but there was no ignoring the screaming coming from across the motel.

Patrick turned to Connor. "Go," he said. "We can handle things here."

Connor nodded and disappeared, the sound of his footsteps receding as he raced back across the landing. Patrick turned to Kurt, nodded, and they continued forward.

He could only hope Connor would reach whoever was screaming in time.

***

"They're clo-o-o-se."

Jason didn't need Chuck to tell him that. He could hear them coming, confident in their mission to find him, not bothering to keep quiet. He smiled at their stupidity, assuring himself that he could not be stopped, that dealing with them would be child's play even though he was outnumbered. He had an advantage over them. He had Chuck.

"Don't get too cocky," the voice in his head said.

Jason nodded in agreement, closed his eyes, and listened. He could hear them, closer now, whispering to each other. They were only two rooms away. He knew that, just as knew that the old man with the shotgun could shoot a hole right through him from a mile away.

"Take the older man out first," Chuck ordered. "The writer can't shoot his own foot even if he tried."

They were close.

Jason opened his eyes and stepped out of the room he was hiding in, immediately raising his gun as he stared into the surprised faces of his pursuers.

*Child's play.*

## Chapter 16

Kurt Layton barely had enough time to react. The deafening sound of the gunshot was quickly followed by a strong blow to his chest, as if someone had taken a swing at him with a giant hammer and had found his mark perfectly. His shoulder screamed as pain raced down his arm and back, the force throwing him off his feet as he spun and fell to the ground.

He could feel blood gushing out from the wound, his heart pounding in his chest as he cried out in pain. The part of him that wasn't trying to understand what had just happened was silently rejoicing to the fact that the bullet hadn't hit him somewhere more fatal. He heard another gunshot, this one closer, and he briefly looked up to see Patrick firing away.

*So much for trying to catch him alive.*

Kurt's lids grew heavy, and the last thing on his mind before he blacked out was how much he had hoped to be the one to kill the crazy bastard.

***

Patrick was screaming in fury.

His first shot missed Jason completely, only startling the man and forcing him to return fire blindly as he raced away. Patrick felt something graze his cheek and swish loudly past his ear, a hot burning sensation spreading quickly across the side of his face. He immediately gave chase, firing another two shots at the man in front of him, wincing at the recoil that numbed his arm.

Jason dashed down the corridor, racing past the first flight of steps and turning swiftly out towards the landing. Patrick tried to keep up, ignoring all sense of caution as he rounded the corner after the man, oblivious to the fact that he was an easy target. Yet he knew that Jason would not stop.

The man was scared. Patrick could feel it, the fear heavy in the air around him as he gave chase. He could sense the man's heartbeats, the gasping breaths, the desire to kill and destroy and conquer. It was like he was in Jason's head, the maniac's thoughts mixed with his own in a psychotic mesh.

Jason jumped over the stair banister, almost falling in his attempt to scale it, and hurried down to the ground floor. Patrick followed close behind, already giving up on trying to fire his gun. He was a lousy shot, and he didn't need to waste any more bullets to prove it.

The rain hit him like an iron fist as he dashed out from the cover of canopy and after Jason. He could barely make out the man's figure through the curtains of water falling from the sky, but he didn't intend to let up. He would follow Jason Collick to the gates of hell if it were the only way to stop him.

The pool gates materialized in front of him, and he watched as Jason slammed against the closed door and stumbled through, pushing to his feet and racing forward. Patrick felt his breaths come in short gasps, the cold air like knives against his throat, but he kept going.

A gunshot echoed through the night, and then another, but Patrick ignored both and kept his eyes on Jason. The man reached the far end of the pool and jumped onto the fence, attempting to climb over it. Patrick was on him in seconds, slamming his body against him, both men bouncing off the fence and falling back onto the ground.

Patrick scrambled onto his hands and knees, frantically looking for the gun he dropped, when a foot connected with his face and sent him rolling. He felt Jason's weight on top of him almost immediately, hands around his neck and squeezing hard. Patrick fought back blindly, rain falling into his eyes and blurring his vision, Jason's weight pinning him down as he slowly suffocated him.

Patrick felt the world around him spin out of focus, the blood in his head pounding as he tried to break free of his attacker's grip. Mustering what little strength he still had, he rolled to the left, and suddenly felt a shock race through him as he was engulfed in the pool's cold waters.

He was in the void again. The darkness, the emptiness, the nothingness. He was suspended in its murkiness, moving in slow motion, kicking out forcefully only to find that he was stuck in his place. He didn't dare breathe, scared that if he did, he would be drawn in and become one with the void. His mind raced, the claustrophobia kicking in once more, and he immediately began to panic. He kicked out, more forcefully this time, and felt the power push him up.

Patrick broke through the surface of the water and gasped for air. His arms flailed as he desperately tried to stay afloat, petrified of sinking back into the darkness he knew he would not be able to escape again. He slapped at the water, kicking out as he looked around frantically, searching for the edge of the pool where he could pull himself out.

A hand grabbed him by the back of his head and pushed him down. The cold water rushed into Patrick's open mouth, forcing him to swallow just so he would drown. He reached up slowly, pushing against the water, and grabbed the hand holding his head down. He pushed it away and kicked back up, gasping as he turned to face his attacker.

Jason Collick had gone completely mad, his eyes wide with rage as he scratched and punched. For a moment, Patrick could have sworn he saw something crawl out of the man's mouth and fall into the water, closely followed by a second and a third. It took him only a second to realize they were little black spiders, more escaping through the man's open mouth, some falling into the water, others crawling up his face and onto his head.

Patrick lashed out, a mix of fear and rage driving him as he grasped Jason by the shoulders, pushed him down and wrapped his arm around the man's neck. Patrick could feel him struggling under the water, writhing about and trying to break free. Dozens of spiders floated on the water's surface, surrounding him as more bubbled out of the drowning man's mouth.

Time passed in slow motion, the storm raging around him as wind and rain increased in intensity, as if the elements themselves wanted to free Jason Collick from his imminent death. Patrick tightened his hold, throwing his weight on top of his captive, cringing at the feel of the spiders on his skin. He cried out into the night, challenging the storm and every other supernatural force that would try to stop him from ending the hell he had had to endure so far.

Jason's efforts to break free weakened, bit by bit, until finally he stopped completely. Patrick unhinged his arm from around the man's neck, and immediately swam towards the edge of the pool and away from the arachnids that lay afloat on the water's surface. He pulled himself out of the water and rolled onto his side, coughing and wheezing, slapping his hand against the ground as he tried to control the pain that enveloped him. From the corner of his eye, he could see Jason's dead body floating in the center of the pool, face down and unmoving.

Patrick rolled onto his back, gazing up at the falling rain as it splattered across his face and into his eyes. The side of his face began to pulse in sync with his heartbeats, and he felt the quick onset of cramps all over his body from the unaccustomed strain he had put his muscles through.

Patrick Lahm closed his eyes and drifted away.

***

Jimmy Frey stood silently in the shadows of the motel's second wing, leaning against the railing as he watched the events at the pool unfold. Tara walked up beside him, her face ashen and blood staining the front of her shirt.

Jimmy glanced at her, then turned away again. "You're hurt."

Tara placed a hand on his shoulder and squeezed. "It's not mine. The old man, Kurt."

"Is he okay?"

Tara didn't answer. Jimmy shifted his concentration back to Patrick.

"I was mistaken about him," Jimmy said. "This is not how I expected it to happen."

Tara squeezed his shoulder again. "Nothing ever is," she reassured him. "I still believe you made the right choice. Only time will tell."

Jimmy nodded, but deep down, he was worried. "It wasn't inside Jason Collick."

"No," Tara whispered. "It wasn't. He was merely a puppet."

"Which makes things that much more complicated."

"It wants Patrick," Tara said. "It won't stop until it has him. For now, we should consider ourselves lucky."

Jimmy pushed away from the railing and followed his mother across the landing to the staircase. They made their way down and crossed through the rain towards the front office.

"How long do I have to stay here?" Jimmy asked.

His mother turned to him and smiled. "If you're right about him, then not for very long," she said.

"You're not coming?"

Tara looked towards the far end of the motel where Patrick lay still by the pool. Another gunshot echoed in the darkness.

"No," she finally said. She bent down to one knee and held her son's face in her hands. "Just remember what's real and what isn't, and soon enough, so will he."

Jimmy felt tears sting his eyes and he quickly brushed them away. He tried his best to smile and hugged his mother tight.

\*\*\*

"Patrick, get up!"

Patrick felt a strong hand shake him, and he slowly opened his eyes. Connor was on one knee beside him, his rifle gripped tight and his frown deep. He was looking in the direction of Owen's apartment, his face a mix of worry and dread.

"Connor?"

Connor looked at him and quickly bent lower, sliding an arm under Patrick and lifting him up.

"Get up," he said frantically. "We need to get out of here! Now!"

Patrick threw an arm around the man's neck and allowed himself to be pulled to his feet, leaning heavily against Connor's large frame.

"What's going on?"

"Everyone's gone completely insane, that's what," Connor said, already moving and dragging Patrick along with him. "We need to leave before things get worse."

Patrick felt weak, his feet sliding across the ground as Connor half-carried him forward.

"Jason's dead," Patrick coughed.

"I can see that," Connor replied, pushing through the pool gates and rushing across the motel parking lot. "So are Owen and Gina, and if we stay any longer, we might just join them."

Patrick looked up at the man in horror, the news almost shocking him to a stop if not for Connor's strength pulling them both along.

"What happened?"

Connor looked over his shoulder, then back as he guided them through the rain. "I have no idea. Owen hung himself in his room, and I shot Gina when she came at me with a knife. I almost shot Harold, too, if Diana hadn't jumped him first. They've all gone frickin' insane!"

Connor guided them to the passenger's side of the truck and stopped, resting the rifle by the door as he opened it for Patrick. "We can't stay here," he said.

Patrick grabbed him by the collar to stop him. "We can't leave," he said. "You know that. You saw what happened when I tried."

"I'm willing to take the risk," Connor said, grabbing Patrick by the waist and heaving him into the passenger seat. "I'm all out of ammunition, and from what I've seen, we're going to need some if we want to survive the night."

Patrick frowned in confusion, unable to come to terms with what he was hearing. It didn't make any sense. He killed Jason. It was supposed to be over. They were supposed to be safe. At least that was what Jimmy had made him believe. He suddenly remembered the boy and his mother, and waited as Connor climbed into the driver's seat to ask him about them.

"I have no clue," Connor said, "and I'm not waiting around to see what happened to them."

A shrill scream cut through the sound of the storm, and both men stared out in horror as they watched a woman race through the rain, chased by a man Patrick knew could only be Harold Bell.

"Is that Diana?" Connor asked.

Patrick had no idea, frozen in his seat as he watched Harold catch up to the woman and grab her by the hair, pulling her down with him as he fell to the ground. The priest was on the woman in an instant, his arms rising and falling as Patrick watched him beat at her relentlessly. The woman kicked and screamed for the briefest of moments before her body went completely still, yet Harold kept going at her.

"Go," Patrick whispered, his voice barely a murmur. "Go, go, go!"

Connor gunned the engine, shifted into drive and pushed down on the gas pedal. He turned the steering wheel hard, the truck skidding on the wet asphalt until he had it speeding towards the motel's exit. Patrick looked back at Harold as the Father continued his assault on the woman, now slamming both his fists down on her in unison. Patrick felt his stomach turn.

"Holy crap!"

Patrick turned back at the sound of surprise in the other man's voice, and stared dumbfounded at Tara and Jimmy standing next to the front office, waving to get their attention.

"Stop," Patrick said.

"No way," Connor said. "I ain't got a death wish."

"Stop!" Patrick yelled, and pulled hard at the handbrake.

The truck skidded dangerously as Connor tried to maintain control, turning the wheel frantically right and left to stop the vehicle from rolling over.

Patrick ignored the angry look on Connor's face and opened his door. He climbed down, lowered the back of his seat and gestured to the Freys. "Get in!" he called out.

Tara and Jimmy raced forward, and Patrick stopped Tara before she climbed in after her son. The woman raised an eyebrow at him questioningly.

"It's still out there, isn't it?" Patrick asked. "It's not over."

Tara looked over her shoulder at the rest of the motel, then back to Patrick. "It is for now," she said, and pulled away from his grip, following her son into the backseat.

Patrick glanced across the motel at Harold. The priest stood motionless over the woman he had beaten to death and stared back at him, and in the darkness beyond, Patrick could see movement. Whatever demons Harold was battling now, they were coming for him, and there was nothing Patrick could do to help him.

"What the hell are you waiting for?" Connor called out.

Patrick climbed back into the truck. He gazed out at the highway beyond the motel's borders and closed his eyes as Connor shifted into drive.

When he opened them again, they had left the Kurtain Motel behind them and were driving north up Route 25.

Chapter 17

Patrick opened his eyes just as the first colors of dawn broke out around them. Before falling asleep, he had doubted their escape, the night still crowding around them and seemingly endless. Now, with the red and orange hues in the skies above, Patrick finally relaxed.

He looked over at Connor, the man's face in a deep frown of concentration, his grip on the wheel tight enough to turn his knuckles white. They were still heading north, well beyond the speed limit, and Patrick reached out to squeeze Connor's shoulder reassuringly.

"Not yet," Connor grumbled, glancing quickly at Patrick before his eyes returned to the road.

Patrick chuckled, adjusting himself in his seat and looking over his shoulder at the passengers in the back. They were both asleep, Jimmy's head resting on his mother's shoulder with his hands crossed over his chest, his eyes moving behind his lids as he dreamed. Patrick sighed, turning back and taking in the rising sun, welcoming the heat and the light. He was happy that the nightmare was finally over.

*You got lucky.*

And he believed it, too. He fought back the images of his struggle with Jason, and tried his best not to admit that the cold feeling racing down his spine was from what he had seen crawling out behind Harold. He shook his head, trying to rid himself of it all. He hadn't been able to see the priest's eyes in the darkness, but he knew that if he had, only madness would have gazed back at him.

Patrick felt a pang of guilt for leaving the man behind. He didn't want to think of Harold as anyone other than the man who had picked him up and offered to help him. He wouldn't have wanted to meet the maniac who had attacked Diana so viciously, so relentlessly. Patrick wondered what would become of the priest now that he was alone in the motel, fighting his own demons, whatever they might be.

\*\*\*

Connor passed two gas stations along their way and voted against stopping at the first town they drove through. He was pushing the truck to the limit, putting as much distance between them and the motel as he possibly could. When the small yellow light underneath the speedometer started to blink, he grudgingly slowed down and ducked into the nearest Mobil.

Jimmy and Tara had woken up a few minutes before, and Patrick noted the look on Jimmy's face at the sight of other people other than the ones they had been hauled up with at the motel. There was hint of excitement there, and a great level of relief. For the first time, Jimmy actually looked like any other normal thirteen-year-old.

"How about you handle the gas while I get us some snacks?" Connor said, already climbing out of the truck.

Patrick nodded as he heard the back door open and close.

"I'll come with you," Tara said, making her way around the front of the truck.

Connor raised an eyebrow and shrugged, giving Patrick a confused look. It was the first time either of them had seen her act in the least bit normal.

"Sure," Connor replied.

Patrick watched as the two made their way to the store, Connor keeping a constant distance between him and Tara and glancing at her every few steps of the way.

"Why?" Patrick asked, watching his two companions disappear behind the glass doors. When he didn't get an answer, he looked back at Jimmy. "Why did we get out?"

Jimmy stared back at him for a few seconds, and he could almost hear the boy's mind searching for the right answer.

"You don't have to sugar coat it for me," Patrick said. "I know the rules don't apply to you and your mother, but you had me believing you knew what you were doing."

"We do," Jimmy replied.

"Then what the hell happened?"

Jimmy looked out his window at the passing traffic, scarce as it was, and shrugged. "Sometimes events take a turn towards the unexpected."

"You messed up," Patrick said. "That's basically what you're saying, right?"

Jimmy looked at him, a dark expression on his face. "We're not always lucky," he said.

Patrick wanted to reply, to tell the boy that luck had nothing to do with any of it. Nobody at the Kurtain Motel had deserved to die, and if he and his mother had been more forthcoming, maybe things would have ended differently. Patrick turned back and shook his head in disbelief. He hated to think what would have happened if Connor hadn't found him and carried him out.

*See, now* that *is lucky.*

Patrick patted for his wallet, took it out and checked to make sure he still had his credit card. He opened his door, gave Jimmy a quick glance, then stepped out to refuel the truck.

***

"Are you sure about this?"

Connor nodded as he drained the last of his water and tossed the empty bottle into the garbage can beside him. Jimmy and Tara sat idly in the backseat, watching the two men talk.

"I need to get home, anyway," Connor said, "and that means heading west."

Patrick nodded and stuck out his hand. The big man curled it in his own and shook hard. "Thanks for everything," Patrick said.

"Don't thank me, yet," Connor said, giving him a weak smile. "Just do me a favor and keep driving. Get the hell out of Connecticut. Hell, if you can make it to Canada, go for it. Just keep going and don't ever look back."

Patrick nodded, fumbling with the keys Connor had given him and glancing back at his passengers. "I think between the three of us, we can figure something out."

Connor nodded, then looked at Patrick seriously. "Listen, I have no idea what happened back there, but something tells me that it's not going to let up. Try to lay low for a while."

"The life of a fugitive," Patrick tried to smile.

"The life of a survivor," Connor replied. "And thanks for the cash. I'll pay you back, somehow."

"Forget about it," Patrick said. "I just hope it gets you where you need to go."

Connor smiled. "Take care of yourself, brother."

He leaned in, gave Patrick a quick hug, and then walked in the opposite direction back to the store. Patrick bounced the keys in his hands as he watched Connor leave, then turned and climbed back into the truck. He could feel Jimmy and Tara's eyes on him, watching as he turned the ignition and shifted into drive. He looked at them through the rear-view mirror, suddenly feeling the weight of his responsibility. He smiled at them.

"Back to the road, guys?"

They didn't reply.

Patrick shrugged, turned on the radio and pulled out of the gas station. He wondered what the weather in Canada would be like this time of year.

* * *

Continue reading with Refuge (The Sin Series Book 2)

## FREE Bonus Novel!

Wow, I hope you enjoyed this book as much as I did writing it! If you enjoyed the book, please leave a review. Your reviews inspire me to continue writing about the world of spooky and untold horrors!

To really show you my appreciation for purchasing this book, please enjoy a **FREE extra spooky bonus novel.** This will surely leave you running scared!

Visit below to download your bonus novel and to learn about my upcoming releases, future discounts and giveaways: www.ScareStreet.com

**FREE books (30 - 60 pages):**
**Ron Ripley (Ghost Stories)**
1. Ghost Stories (Short Story Collection)
   www.scarestreet.com/ghost

**A.I. Nasser (Supernatural Suspense)**
2. Polly's Haven (Short Story)
   www.scarestreet.com/pollys
3. This is Gonna Hurt (Short Story)
   www.scarestreet.com/thisisgonna

**Multi-Author Scare Street Collaboration**
4. Horror Stories: A Short Story Collection
   www.scarestreet.com/horror

And experience the full-length novels (150 – 210 pages):
**Ron Ripley (Ghost Stories)**
1. Sherman's Library Trilogy (FREE via mailing list signup)
   www.scarestreet.com
2. The Boylan House Trilogy
   www.scarestreet.com/boylantri
3. The Blood Contract Trilogy
   www.scarestreet.com/bloodtri

4. The Enfield Horror Trilogy
   www.scarestreet.com/enfieldtri

## Moving In Series

5. **Moving In Series Box Set Books 1 - 3 (22% off)**
   www.scarestreet.com/movinginbox123
6. Moving In (Book 1)
   www.scarestreet.com/movingin
7. The Dunewalkers (Moving In Series Book 2)
   www.scarestreet.com/dunewalkers
8. Middlebury Sanitarium (Book 3)
   www.scarestreet.com/middlebury
9. **Moving In Series Box Set Books 4 - 6 (25% off)**
   www.scarestreet.com/movinginbox456
10. The First Church (Book 4)
    www.scarestreet.com/firstchurch
11. The Paupers' Crypt (Book 5)
    www.scarestreet.com/paupers
12. The Academy (Book 6)
    www.scarestreet.com/academy

## Berkley Street Series

13. Berkley Street (Book 1)
    www.scarestreet.com/berkley
14. The Lighthouse (Book 2)
    www.scarestreet.com/lighthouse
15. The Town of Griswold (Book 3)
    www.scarestreet.com/griswold
16. Sanford Hospital (Book 4)
    www.scarestreet.com/sanford
17. Kurkow Prison (Book 5)
    www.scarestreet.com/kurkow
18. Lake Nutaq (Book 6)
    www.scarestreet.com/nutaq
19. Slater Mill (Book 7)
    www.scarestreet.com/slater
20. Borgin Keep (Book 8)
    www.scarestreet.com/borgin
21. Amherst Burial Ground (Book 9)
    www.scarestreet.com/amherst

## Hungry Ghosts Street Series

## David Longhorn (Supernatural Suspense)
## The Sentinels Series
37. Sentinels (Book 1)
   www.scarestreet.com/sentinels
38. The Haunter (Book 2)
   www.scarestreet.com/haunter
39. The Smog (Book 3)
   www.scarestreet.com/smog
## Dark Isle Series
40. Dark Isle (Book 1)
   www.scarestreet.com/darkisle
41. White Tower (Book 2)
   www.scarestreet.com/whitetower
42. The Red Chapel (Book 3)
   www.scarestreet.com/redchapel
## Ouroboros Series
43. The Sign of Ouroboros (Book 1)
   www.scarestreet.com/ouroboros
44. Fortress of Ghosts (Book 2)
   www.scarestreet.com/fortress
45. Day of The Serpent (Book 3)
   www.scarestreet.com/serpent
## Curse of Weyrmouth Series
46. Curse of Weyrmouth (Book 1)
   www.scarestreet.com/weyrmouth
47. Blood of Angels (Book 2)
   www.scarestreet.com/bloodofangels

## Eric Whittle (Psychological Horror)
## Catharsis Series
48. Catharsis (Book 1)
   www.scarestreet.com/catharsis
49. Mania (Book 2)
   www.scarestreet.com/mania
50. Coffer (Book 3)
   www.scarestreet.com/coffer
## Sara Clancy (Supernatural Suspense)
## Dark Legacy Series

51. Black Bayou (Book 1)
    www.scarestreet.com/bayou
52. Haunted Waterways (Book 2)
    www.scarestreet.com/waterways
53. Demon's Tide (Book 3)
    www.scarestreet.com/demonstide

**Banshee Series**

54. Midnight Screams (Book 1)
    www.scarestreet.com/midnight
55. Whispering Graves (Book 2)
    www.scarestreet.com/whispering
56. Shattered Dreams (Book 3)
    www.scarestreet.com/shattered

**Black Eyed Children Series**

57. Black Eyed Children (Book 1)
    www.scarestreet.com/blackeyed
58. Devil's Rise (Book 2)
    www.scarestreet.com/rise
59. The Third Knock (Book 3)
    www.scarestreet.com/thirdknock

**Demonic Games Series**

60. Demonic Games (Book 1)
    www.scarestreet.com/nesting
61. Buried (Book 2)
    www.scarestreet.com/buried

**Chelsey Dagner (Supernatural Suspense)**
**Ghost Mirror Series**

62. Ghost Mirror (Book 1)
    www.scarestreet.com/ghostmirror
63. The Gatekeeper (Book 2)
    www.scarestreet.com/gatekeeper

**See you in the shadows,**
**Team Scare Street**

CPSIA information can be obtained
at www.ICGtesting.com
Printed in the USA
LVHW080549200420
654105LV00011B/1385